Janet steadied the ladder with one hand and hugged the fishbowl with the other while Nicky climbed up to Mrs. Cooper's kitchen window. She looked down at the snake, coiled up and eyeing her steadily. She decided it might be safer to carry the snake up without the bowl. She set the bowl down on the grass.

Nicky carefully removed the screen. The window started to drop, but he held it open. The white ruffled curtains fluttered in the breeze. "Hurry up," he said. "I can't hold this thing forever."

Janet looked down at the snake, held her breath, and grabbed it right below the head. It felt colder than she expected, and she almost dropped it. Quickly, she mounted the rungs, holding the snake out in front of her. She tiptoed across the shingles and up to where Nicky was waiting.

"Okay, stick it in!" said Nicky.

Janet thrust her hand inside the curtains and let go of the snake. Nicky slapped the screen back into place and let the window drop.

They looked at each other. "Done!" said Janet. "Let's get out of here."

They put the ladder back in the shed and were hurrying across the backyard when the screen door flew open. "Janet!" yelled Donnie. "That lady's here! Mrs. Cooper's daughter!"

**Be sure to read all of the
books in the Chronicles
of Courage series:**

A Better Tomorrow?

Operation Morningstar

Gold in the Garden

A Better Tomorrow?

A Better Tomorrow?

Dorothy Lilja Harrison

Chariot VICTOR
PUBLISHING
A DIVISION OF COOK COMMUNICATIONS

Chariot Books
is an imprint of ChariotVictor Publishing, division of Cook
Communications, Colorado Springs, Colorado 80918
Cook Communications, Paris, Ontario
Kingsway Communications, Eastbourne, England

A BETTER TOMORROW?
© 1997 by Dorothy Lilja Harrison

Cover design by Rick A. Mills
Cover illustration by Ron Mazellan

First printing, 1997
Printed in the United States of America
01 00 99 98 97   5 4 3 2 1

In memory of my mother and father,
who knew that there would be
a better tomorrow.

Table of Contents

Acknowledgments

My special thanks to my editor, Sue Reck, whose wish for broader brushstrokes helped to enlarge and, hopefully, improve this story.

I am grateful also for the insights of my fellow children's writers, without whose encouragement my books might never have been submitted for publication.

Chapter 1

1934

Mrs. Cooper's Rules

"No loud noises in the house! No walking on the grass in the front yard! No playing on the front porch!"

Still in their pajamas, Janet and Donnie sat upright on the couch as their new landlady counted off the rules on her bony fingers, peering at them over wire-rimmed glasses. Mrs. Cooper's high-collared dress and laced-up shoes reminded Janet of the faded pictures of her grandmother. Unlike her grandmother, though, Mrs. Cooper's face was as stiff as her collar.

"No ball-playing in the backyard!" the landlady continued. "The last children who lived here broke my kitchen window!" She rolled her eyes heavenward.

Humph! thought Janet. Who could play ball in her dumb little yard, anyway?

Then came the fifth rule: "And no friends in the house or yard on Sundays!"

Donnie looked over at Mama. "Are cousins friends?" he asked, twisting a lock of his hair. Their cousins had always come over on Sundays when they lived in Columbia Heights. Janet and Donnie thought those boys were more fun than anyone.

Mrs. Cooper made it clear: "No children visiting on Sundays. That is the Sabbath, and I cannot have a day of rest with children running about."

Mama stiffened in her chair and started to say something, but Papa interrupted her. "Vee understand, Mrs. Cooper," he said, looking sternly at Mama, "and vee'll see that our children do, too."

The landlady nodded, gripping her ivory-handled cane with hands that were crisscrossed with purple veins. "Good," she said, rising. "I've rented these rooms to several families over the past few years, Mr. Larson, and the ones who just moved out of here . . . well, things just didn't work out, so they had to be evicted."

Mama looked over at Papa in alarm.

Mrs. Cooper continued, "Now mind you, I know that children have to play, but . . . well, I don't understand what gets into youngsters nowadays. When I was raising mine, children were to be seen and not heard!" The landlady leaned forward and looked straight at Janet and Donnie. "What I want to say is that you are welcome to stay in my house as long as you follow the rules." With that, she excused herself and returned to her upstairs apartment.

"What's a-victed?" asked Donnie, as soon as Papa shut the door.

"Evicted," corrected Papa. He wearily crossed the living room and opened the door of the stove. "People get evicted ven they can't pay their rent," he said solemnly, stirring the glowing coals with a poker, "or ven they disobey the rules." He closed the black iron door firmly and stood the poker against the stove. Then he faced the children.

"They come and move the furniture right out of the house."

Donnie sat wide-eyed, and Janet nodded. "Like the Blakes," she said. Back in Columbia Heights, Janet had come home from school with Irene Blake one day, and everything the family owned was on the sidewalk. Even Irene's dolls. That was last year, when she and Janet had just started fourth grade. Janet never saw the Blakes after that, but someone said they went to Milwaukee.

Mama turned to Papa. She spoke softly, but with clenched fists. "How can we live here with three lively children and abide by rules like that?"

"It's not a question of how, Anna," said Papa, shaking his head. "Vee must! Where else can vee go?" Papa had been out of work ever since his grocery store had to close last year. Finding a place they could afford—even in a Polish neighborhood in Minneapolis—had not been easy. Janet remembered how Mama had cried when he first told her that's where they were moving.

Donnie's lower lip quivered. "I wanna go back to Columbia Heights," he said.

Then Mama and Papa started speaking Swedish to each other. They did that whenever they didn't want their children to know what they were talking about. Mama hadn't come from Sweden like Papa, but Mama's parents had, and she had learned Swedish at Sunday School. Janet had vowed that someday she would learn to speak Swedish, too, even though Papa said that American children didn't need to learn it anymore.

Papa pulled his jacket from the hook behind the stove and shoved his arms into the sleeves. "There's still some stuff in the driveway," he said. "I've got to put it in the garage before it starts snowing again."

Mama hoisted two-year-old Patty onto her hip and

headed back to the kitchen with Donnie in tow. Janet followed.

"Mama," whined Donnie, "we don't have to do everything Mrs. Cooper says, do we?"

"Of course we do. You heard your father." Mama put Patty into her high chair.

"We can't even have our cousins here?" asked Janet, tying her sister's flannel bib under her chin. She gave Patty a piece of dry toast. "Not ever?"

Mama returned to the things she had been unpacking. "No children on Sundays," she said, bending down. Her voice came up from the depths of the barrel. "You heard what Mrs. Cooper said."

"But Mama, that's the only day they can ever come over!" Janet stood with her hands on her hips.

Mama straightened up and sighed. "They'll just have to come on Saturdays."

"Uncle Ed's always busy on Saturdays." Janet could feel her eyes starting to fill up. Papa's car had broken down, and with no money to fix it, Uncle Ed was their only link to Cambridge, where his family lived. And Cambridge was an hour's drive away.

Mama had been carefully unwrapping dishes from a barrel before Mrs. Cooper arrived. Now, though, she had reached the pans, and each time she brought one up, she yanked off the newspaper and slammed the pan on the table. "Better eat your breakfast," she said, bending back down. "I want to get the dishes done."

Janet frowned and took two bowls from the stack on the oilcloth-covered table. She poured cornflakes into each bowl and shoved one toward Donnie, who sat opposite, fiddling with a spoon.

"You'll have to get your milk from the icebox," said

Mama, rising. "I haven't found the pitcher yet." She set another pan on the end of the table, pushed her blond hair out of her eyes and sighed. Janet wished she had blond hair like her brother and sister, but Mama said Janet got her hair from her father. She never understood how that worked, but at least she had Papa's blue eyes, too, and sometimes people said they were pretty.

The Larsons had brought their icebox with them from Columbia Heights. The wooden box, about as high as Janet, had a top section and a bottom section. The only thing in the top was a big chunk of ice that cooled the food on the shelves below.

Janet opened the icebox door and carefully lifted a milk bottle from the dark interior. She dribbled some milk into each bowl, replaced the cardboard cap, and set the heavy bottle back on the cold shelf. Mama always said not to leave milk bottles on the table like the Polacks do.

Donnie was sprinkling sugar on his cereal. His tousled hair hung down over his eyes. He never combed it unless Mama reminded him. "I just figgered out something," he said. "This is a used-to-be house."

"What do you mean?" asked Janet, reaching for the sugar.

"Well, you know how Mama and Papa's bedroom used to be a sun porch? Well, I bet the living room used to be the dining room, and your bedroom used to be the living room!" Then he pointed at the ceiling. "And that lady used to live in the whole house."

"Her name is Mrs. Cooper," said Janet.

Donnie pushed back his cereal bowl and wiped his mouth on his pajama sleeve. "Well, whatever it is, I don't like her," he said, sliding down from his chair.

"Shhh! Not so loud, Donnie," said Mama. "You're

going to have to be nice to her." Donnie had left the room, but Mama kept talking. "We were lucky to be able to rent this place." She looked absently toward the window. "God knows we can't afford anything else."

Janet sat watching her mother. Mama's flowered cotton housedress drooped from her bony shoulders like a sack, but her faded apron held the dress tightly around her waist. "Did you eat, Mama?" Janet asked soberly.

"Not yet. I'll get something later," answered Mama from down in the barrel, but Janet knew she wouldn't. Papa scolded Mama for skipping meals, but she did it anyway. She did it to save food; Janet knew that.

Janet stacked the dirty bowls and carried them over to the sink. "Mama," she said, "President Roosevelt's going to fix it so people can get jobs again. My teacher said so."

Mama threw her chin forward. "Fourteen million people out of work and Roosevelt's going to find jobs for all of them? He can't do that for all the tea in China! A lot of people got us into this mess, and it's going to take more than one man to get us out of it!" She looked absently toward the window again. "So we're stuck here for heaven knows how long."

Patty started banging on the high chair tray. Janet silently wiped her face, untied her bib, and lifted her down from the chair. After her sister toddled into the living room, Janet pulled her up on her lap in the high-backed rocking chair. She pressed her cheek against Patty's wispy blond hair, hugging her as they rocked.

Through a wide doorway, Janet could see the bed she now had to share with her sister because the crib wouldn't fit anywhere in the house. Patty had slept on the side of the bed that was pushed against the wall.

A cardboard box sat in a shadowy corner next to the

dresser. Janet had packed it carefully before Papa and Uncle Ed loaded the truck. Inside were her drawings, three pencils and an art gum eraser, a stack of baseball cards bound with a rubber band, and *Alice's Adventures in Wonderland,* her very own book.

On top of these treasures was her empty fishbowl, which Janet had wrapped in an old shirt so it wouldn't break during the bouncy move. They couldn't afford another goldfish, but Janet was going to keep the bowl anyway. Papa said this whole business—leaving Columbia Heights and living here—was only temporary. Someday soon the Depression would be over, he'd said, and Janet could get some more fish. The fishbowl would remind Janet of Papa's promise.

Meanwhile, though, there was Mrs. Cooper and her awful rules. *Well,* thought Janet, rocking faster, *no rules are going to stop me from having friends. Not even Mrs. Cooper's.*

Chapter 2

1934

Neighbors

The next morning while Janet was washing the breakfast dishes, someone knocked on the door. She wiped her hands and opened it slightly. Three boys in heavy wool jackets were lined up on the back porch, hugging themselves against the cold. They were about her age, ten or eleven.

"Hi!" said the tallest boy, smiling down at her. Janet could see his breath as he talked. "Saw you moving in yesterday. Just wondered if you've got any brothers."

"One," said Janet, "but he's only six." She smiled and stepped aside. "My name's Janet. Want to come in?"

"Naw, never mind," said one of the boys, turning to leave.

But the tall one said, "Maybe for a minute or two." He grinned at the others and cocked his head toward the door. "Come on, you guys," he said.

They stepped inside, pulled off their leather helmets and waited, looking around at the kitchen. The taller boy ran long fingers through his dark curly hair. "I'm Eddie Polzac," he said. "I live next door." His broad smile put Janet at ease. He nudged the boy on his right. "This is Nicky Rusinsky."

Nicky tossed back a shock of straight dark hair and nodded.

"And this," said Eddie, poking the other boy, "is Butch Butowski."

Butch's freckles reminded Janet of her friend Mike back in Columbia Heights. "Hi," they said to each other, grinning. Butch was about the same height as Janet.

Donnie came humming through the living room doorway, but stopped when he saw the boys.

"This is Donnie," said Janet. "My brother."

The boys smiled at him, and then Eddie said to Janet, "Your landlady told us there were three kids in your family. Who's the other one?"

"Patty," said Donnie, waving a paper airplane. "She's a baby."

Janet smiled at Eddie. "Too bad we don't have any boys your age," she said. She decided to change the subject. "You like bubble gum baseball cards?" she asked. "I've been collecting them since I was a little kid. Got a hundred and sixty-nine. Wanna see them?"

In a few minutes everyone was busily examining the cards, which Janet had spread over the kitchen table. The boys didn't seem to mind that most of them were faded and worn.

"Look," said Butch, "she's got Hank Greenberg! Wow! Best first baseman the Tigers ever had!"

"Yeah, but not as good as Lou Gehrig," said Nicky, slapping down another card. "Forty-nine home runs, a hundred and sixty-five RBIs, and a three sixty-three batting average! Can't beat those Yankees!"

Janet grinned triumphantly. Alongside Lou Gehrig she placed another hefty player, shouldering a bat. "Babe Ruth!" she exclaimed. "Champion outfielder!" The boys glanced at each other and back at Janet in admiration.

Eddie spoke up. "The Babe's the best hitter in baseball. Over seven hundred home runs so far."

"That's what I mean about the Yankees," said Nicky. "They're all-time champs. No question!"

Butch sat fingering one of the cards. "Wish I had a collection like this. Haven't bought any bubble gum in months."

Janet nodded, her smile fading as she began to slide the cards into a stack. It would probably be a long time before she'd be buying any new ones either.

Eddie suddenly asked, "Hey, Janet, you gonna go to public or Catholic?"

"What?" she replied.

"School. You gonna go to St. Jerome's?"

She shook her head. "We're going to Howard. Papa says it's up at the end of the street, but I haven't seen it yet."

"Well," said Eddie, "at least we can see each other after school."

Nicky handed Janet the rest of the cards. "You got any pets?" he asked.

Janet shook her head again. "We had a cat, but she got run over. My goldfish died, too, but I'm gonna get another one—someday."

"Eddie's got a white mouse," said Butch, leaning on the table with his elbows.

"You do?" asked Janet, her eyes brightening.

Eddie grinned. "Yup. He got loose in the house once, and my mother almost croaked. I really have to watch him now, or she'll make me get rid of him."

"Can I see him?" asked Janet, slipping a rubber band around the cards. "Sometime, I mean."

"Now's okay, if you want to. Can you come over?"

"Soon as I finish the dishes!"

A few minutes later Janet was knocking on Eddie's back door. Eddie let her in and introduced her to his older brother, George, and to his mother, who was kneading dough at the kitchen table. George looked a lot like Eddie, but he was about a foot taller.

Mrs. Polzac paused at her kneading. "So you're the oldest girl," she said, smiling. Her dark hair was streaked with gray, and she had flour on the end of her nose. "I saw your mother and the little ones yesterday," she continued, folding the pile of shiny dough. "Glad to have you as neighbors."

"Hope you stay longer than the Turners did," said George.

Mrs. Polzac gave George a stern glance and then looked back at Janet. "That's the family who used to live in your house."

"I know," said Janet. "Mrs. Cooper told us about them yesterday." Then she added slowly, "She said she had to evict them."

There was an awkward pause. Eddie's mother pushed on the dough with her palms and then folded it again quickly. Janet watched, fascinated, as first her palms and then her fingers kept up the rhythm.

"I'll never forget the day I came back from Mass," Mrs. Polzac continued, "and all their furniture was piled up on the sidewalk. Sorriest sight I ever saw!" She stopped, lowering her voice. "Don't cause any trouble for that woman. She's . . . well, just be sure not to get her upset!"

She lifted the dough, folded it over one last time, and slipped it into a large buttered bowl. She carried the bowl over to the stove as Eddie and Janet turned to leave the room.

"Eddie," his mother called out over her shoulder, "don't forget, you've got to leave for confession by 10:30. Don't want you late again."

"Yeah, Mom," said Eddie. He led Janet down into the basement, where he kept his mouse.

"Nice cage," said Janet, leaning over for a closer look at the white ball sleeping in wood shavings. "What's his name?"

"Mickey."

Janet smiled. "No better name for a mouse!"

"Wanna pet him?"

"Sure."

Eddie swung open the wire cage top, and Janet reached in and stroked Mickey's warm fur. "I thought maybe you'd be afraid of him," said Eddie, watching.

"Well, I've never actually petted a mouse before, but we had a guinea pig at my school in Columbia Heights, and I used to help clean the cage." Janet smiled again, remembering. "We took turns holding him. Of course, guinea pigs don't run away like mice do." She closed the cage. "What do you feed him?" she asked.

By the time they left the house, Janet knew almost as much about keeping mice as she did about guinea pigs. She and Eddie stepped through the drifted snow and into her side yard just as Nicky and Butch came up the street. When the boys saw Eddie and Janet, they ran up the sloping bank to meet them.

Janet clapped a mittened hand over her mouth. "Don't do that!" she said.

"Do what?" asked Nicky.

"Don't run up the bank. Mrs. Cooper doesn't allow it."

"We didn't hurt nothin'," said Butch.

"I know, but she's really strict. Our family can get into big trouble if we disobey her rules."

"Yeah," said Eddie. "They could get evicted!"

Janet winced as they all glanced up at Mrs. Cooper's curtained window.

Butch rolled his eyes. "Old Lady Cooper's the one that oughta go to confession!"

Eddie winked at Janet. "We've gotta go," he said, and the boys turned and stepped daintily down the steps to the sidewalk.

"Tiptoe—through the tulips . . ." they sang, with silly grins on their faces.

Janet stood giggling and then turned to go inside, wishing suddenly that she were Catholic, too.

Just as she mounted the steps, the front door opened slowly, and Mrs. Cooper stepped out with a canvas shopping bag draped over her arm. She stopped next to Janet and placed two silver-wrapped chocolates onto her mitten. "Sweets for the Swede," she smiled, continuing down the steps. Then she turned and peered at Janet. "What were those boys doing here?" she asked.

"I just met them."

The landlady sniffed. "They're Polacks, you know."

"What?"

"Polacks. They've taken over the neighborhood." She hobbled down the walk, calling over her shoulder, "It's not like it used to be around here."

Janet stood and squeezed her mitten around the silver candy as the landlady continued up the street. *Well,* she thought, *if Eddie's a Polack, then I'm glad Polacks live here.* She dropped one of the chocolates into her pocket and quickly unwrapped the other. She slipped it into her mouth, grateful that Donnie wasn't around, or she'd have to share the other one with him. It had been weeks since they'd had candy, let alone chocolates. Maybe Mrs. Cooper wouldn't be so awful after all.

Just as she turned to go inside, a familiar truck came chugging up the street. It was Uncle Ed, and the cousins were inside, waving at her!

Chapter 3

1934

The Cousins

The truck had barely come to a stop along the curb when Jack and Tommy jumped out. "Last one up the steps is a rotten egg!" said Jack, pushing ahead of his brother. They disappeared inside the house before Uncle Ed had gotten out of the cab. Janet waited for him on the sidewalk.

"Your Aunt Edith couldn't come," said Uncle Ed, handing Janet a newspaper-wrapped bundle, "but she baked this casserole for your dinner tonight."

Janet smiled. "That was nice of her," she said. "Mama's so busy unpacking." She cradled the warm package in her arms and carefully mounted the steps.

"So, you like the new place?" Uncle Ed asked. He had seen the house the day before, when he helped them move in.

Janet shrugged her shoulders. "It's okay."

"Lucky you're not living upstairs, like vee are." Uncle Ed always huffed and puffed up staircases. Papa had said he should lose some weight, but Janet liked him the way he was. He reminded her of Santa Claus—no beard, but just as jolly.

Jack and Tommy were busy playing tiddlywinks with Donnie by the time Janet got inside. "They never waste a minute," said Mama, smiling, as she set the casserole on the kitchen stove. "Where do they get their energy?"

"Oh, I yust vind them up every morning!" said Uncle Ed, winking at Janet.

Mama put on the coffeepot, and soon everyone was chattering around the kitchen table.

Janet remembered how Mama used to fix cocoa for the kids, but now all they could have was milk and a soda cracker. She thought about the silver-wrapped chocolates Mrs. Cooper had given her and was glad she'd had time to eat one. She decided to eat the other later, when no one was looking.

Papa told Uncle Ed how he'd been looking and looking for work but couldn't find any. Uncle Ed said maybe he ought to try Milwaukee or Chicago.

Janet froze. Milwaukee or Chicago! That would be hundreds of miles away. And she didn't want to move again.

"Vell, I vould go yust by myself," responded Papa, when Janet said she didn't want to move.

"But who would take care of us?" asked Donnie, twisting a lock of his hair.

"Your mama, of course," said Papa, patting him on the head playfully, but he was looking at his wife.

Mama frowned and shoved her hands deep into her apron pockets. "That's awfully far away, Karl," she said.

"I know, but I vouldn't have to be gone long, yust long enough to make a little money."

Mama's face brightened when Papa mentioned

money. Then she frowned again. "But where would you stay?" she said.

Uncle Ed spoke up. "If he vent to Chicago, maybe he could stay vith Sven and Millie." Uncle Sven was Papa's oldest brother, but because they lived so far away, Janet had never met him or Aunt Millie. Janet couldn't imagine Papa staying with people she didn't even know.

"Vell," said Papa, "I'll yust have to see."

Uncle Ed sat stirring his coffee with his spoon. Suddenly he looked over at Papa. "The vay things are going at the plant," he said, "I may be looking for vork myself pretty soon."

Mama's cup clattered onto her saucer. "No, Ed! Not you, too!"

Uncle Ed nodded sadly.

"If that happens," said Papa, putting an arm around his brother, "vee'll go looking together."

Janet shuddered. She didn't want to think about Papa ever leaving, and she was glad when the cousins asked to see her baseball cards.

"They're in my desk," she said, jumping up from the table. The boys all followed her, with Patty toddling after.

As they were leaving the kitchen, Mama said, "Be sure to keep your voices down."

Janet grinned and called over her shoulder, "Don't worry. Mrs. Cooper went shopping."

Then she heard Papa say, "Yah, and she's liable to come back any minute."

As Janet spread her baseball cards out on the double bed, she told the cousins about Mrs. Cooper's rules.

"She sounds awful," said Jack.

"She is," said Donnie. "She might avict us."

"E-vict, Donnie," said Janet. She looked back at her

cousins. "She won't as long as we obey her rules."

The boys nodded that they understood, but a few minutes later, when Tommy pulled a card from Jack's hand, Jack punched him in the side. Tommy yelled and hit Jack harder. Soon they were on the floor punching each other. Patty became frightened and started to cry.

Uncle Ed came in and stopped the fight, and Mama took Patty out of the room. But just then there was a loud thump-thump overhead.

"Mrs. Cooper!" said Donnie, pointing up. He grinned. "That's her wooden leg." The cousins looked up, wide-eyed.

"She doesn't have a wooden leg!" laughed Janet, and the boys all joined in.

Papa appeared in the doorway, looking cross. "Shhh!" he said, and then he said softly, "That vas probably Mrs. Cooper's cane. Ven she bangs it on her floor, it means be quiet!"

Janet rolled her eyes, but they all played quietly after that.

Too soon it was time for Uncle Ed and the boys to return to Cambridge. At the door, Uncle Ed said, "Vee can come back a veek from Sunday."

Mama and Papa looked at each other. "Vill the boys be along?" asked Papa, stroking his chin.

"Oh, yah, and Edith, too," said Uncle Ed, smiling.

So Papa had to tell him about the landlady's "No Children on Sundays" rule. Uncle Ed shook his head and said they'd try for a Saturday, but he wasn't sure just when.

Janet bit her lip. *Dumb, stupid old Mrs. Cooper,* she thought. *We can't have any fun around here.* But then she thought, *maybe without Uncle Ed around, Papa will forget about leaving.*

New Kid in Class

On Monday morning, Papa stayed home with Patty while Mama went with Janet and Donnie to their new school. The snowplow had left small white mountains along the sidewalk on Washington Street and a path just wide enough for them to walk single file. All the way along the five blocks, Donnie pretended he was an Indian following Mama. Janet lagged behind both of them, dreading to be a new kid at Howard Elementary.

When they stopped at a corner, Mama turned to her and asked, "Why are you so poky, Janet?"

She looked away. "I dunno," she said.

"She wants to be a Catholic," said Donnie.

Mama's eyebrows jumped. "What?"

Janet swung her elbow at Donnie. "I didn't say that." Then she looked over at her mother. "I just wish Eddie and Nicky went to Howard and not a Catholic school. Then I'd know somebody there."

Mama said, "It's better they have their own schools."

Janet didn't know what she meant by that, and she didn't feel like asking.

The gray stone school building was surrounded by a paved yard partially covered by snow. The yard was encircled by a high chain-link fence. Inside the fence, dozens of children stood around stamping their feet in the cold, waiting for the bell to ring, while others just chased each other about. Across the school yard, Janet could see the metal frames for swings and seesaws, bare and deserted now in the dead of winter.

As they walked through the wide gate, Donnie asked, "Is the fence to keep people out or kids in?"

"Neither right now," smiled Mama, "but maybe they lock the gate sometimes when school is closed."

Janet was glad they had to go right into the office. She didn't want to stay outside with all those kids looking at her. By the time she arrived at her classroom later, though, all the fifth graders were at their desks, and a gray-haired woman with glasses was standing by the door. "Good morning," she said, patting Janet on the shoulder. "I'm Miss Jamison. Welcome to Howard School."

Janet flashed a smile and pulled nervously at her worn sleeves. The teacher helped Janet find a hook for her coat in the small cloakroom just outside the classroom. The cloakroom was crowded with wet wool jackets, and discarded galoshes lay in little puddles on the wooden floor.

Janet followed Miss Jamison inside, trying to ignore all the eyes that were fastened on her. The teacher introduced her to the children and pointed to an empty desk near the front of the room. "You may sit up there next to Elaine Carlson," she said.

Janet made her way up the aisle to the empty desk next to a girl with long blond curls. The girl smiled at her as she sank down onto the seat, grateful to blend in with the other children.

The small wooden desk and its separate, flip-up seat had iron legs that were bolted to the floor, as were all the other desks in the room. Janet carefully lifted the hinged desktop and peeked inside. It was empty. So was the inkwell. A bottle of ink should have been in the hole at the upper right corner of the desk. Scratched into the top were sets of initials of kids who had used the desk before Janet. The largest pair looked as if they'd been gouged out with a knife. Janet remembered Mama's quote:

> Fools' names, like fools' faces,
> Are often seen in public places.

When the teacher passed out geography books, Elaine showed Janet where to start reading. Later, when they worked on penmanship, Elaine said, "We can share my ink bottle until Miss Jamison finds one for you." Janet smiled and thought, *I guess I won't miss Eddie and Nicky so much after all.*

Dipping her pen carefully so she wouldn't splash any ink drops, Janet copied her letters slowly, first the capitals and then the small letters. Miss Jamison, checking on her pupils, stopped at Janet's desk. "I see you're left-handed," she said, smiling.

Janet nodded.

"Then your paper should be turned around," she said, turning it for Janet as she spoke. "Left-handed writing," she continued, "should slant backward."

Janet looked up and grinned, but after the teacher had moved on, she turned her paper back the way she had it before. She had to curve her hand above her work to write her way, and that made it look right-handed, but that was how she had always written. Janet swallowed hard, remembering her teacher back in Columbia Heights. *She would never have turned my paper around like that*, she thought.

When everyone left the building for lunch, Elaine walked part of the way home with Janet and Donnie. "How far down on Washington Street do you live?" Elaine asked, stopping in front of her own house. Donnie told her, and she said, "That's not Mrs. Cooper's house, is it?"

"Yeah," said Janet. "Why?"

Elaine shrugged. "I used to know someone who lived there, that's all."

"What was her name?"

"Oh, it was Doris," said Elaine, looking off. "She used to be in our class."

"Doris who?" asked Janet. "What was her last name?"

"Turner."

That was it, thought Janet—*the name of the family Eddie's mother had told her about.* The ones who got evicted. Janet could feel her heart pounding. "What happened to her?" she asked, dreading the answer.

"I don't know," said Elaine. "She was at school one day, and the next day she was gone. Just like that." She clapped her mittened hands together.

Janet shuddered. She could still hear Mrs. Cooper telling Mama and Papa how that family had to be evicted. *Maybe that really could happen to us*, she thought. *But then again, maybe they did some awful things or something . . .*

Two days later, the teacher passed out watercolor paint boxes to everyone in class. Janet spent the next hour happily painting the bowl of oranges that Miss Jamison had placed on a cloth-covered table. She'd told them they were making a "still life" when they painted flowers in a vase or fruit.

The teacher walked slowly up the aisle to see what each of her pupils were painting. When she got to Janet's desk, she said, "I like the way you've caught the roundness of the oranges, Janet," she said. "They look so real."

Janet blushed and kept working.

Joey Barnhart, who sat in front of Janet, turned around and said, "Hey, look at the artist." The boy next to him snickered, but Miss Jamison glared at them and said that all famous artists start out first as children. Janet and Elaine smiled at each other, and when the teacher wasn't looking, Elaine stuck her tongue out at Joey.

A few days later Miss Jamison told the children there was to be a poster contest for the fifth and sixth graders. The posters were to remind everyone at Howard to bring in cans of food for the poor. Those who wanted to make one should raise their hands, and she would give them a large piece of paper to take home so they could start working on it. Janet wanted to make one, but she didn't dare raise her hand. She shot a glance over at Elaine, who already had her hand up.

Elaine smiled. "Go ahead, Janet," she whispered. "You could make a good one!"

Janet grinned. "You really think so?"

"Sure!"

Janet slowly raised her hand. Miss Jamison beamed and headed up the aisle. "The one who makes the best poster," she said, handing Elaine and Janet their papers, "will get a surprise gift."

Janet proudly carried home her rolled-up poster paper and told her parents all about the contest. Mama said Janet could use the kitchen table to work on it until dinner.

"What are the posters for?" asked Mama, stirring macaroni as it boiled on the woodstove.

"To tell everyone to bring in canned goods for the poor," said Janet.

Mama put her hand over her mouth and then dropped it. "Canned goods for the poor . . ." she said quietly. She turned back to the stove and shook her head.

"Yep," said Janet, leaning over her work. "They're going to put the best posters up in the hall, and the one who makes the best one wins a prize!"

Donnie joined Janet at the table. "I want to make a poster, too!" he said.

"You can't," said Janet. "First graders are too little, and besides, you have to have special paper." She kept on drawing.

Donnie pouted. "Well, I could make one if I had some!"

Mama reached up and tore the January 1934 page off the kitchen calendar. "Here, Donnie," she said, "tomorrow's February, so we won't need this anymore."

Donnie grabbed it and climbed back up on his chair.

Janet narrowed her eyes. "That's not fair, Mama. Donnie got the calendar page last month, too!"

Mama sighed. "Well, you can have it next time, Janet," she said. "For goodness' sake, stop complaining. You have that nice poster paper."

Janet turned back to Donnie. "You still can't be in the contest," she said.

Donnie stuck out his chin. "I don't care. This poster's gonna be for our house!" He flipped the calendar page over and started drawing.

Janet watched out of the corner of her eye as Donnie hurried through his picture. It looked something like Janet's, with a stack of canned goods, but Donnie's cans were all crooked. *And he doesn't know*, thought Janet, smiling to herself, *that I'm going to put smiles on all my cans.* She kept on drawing carefully so that each of her cans would look as real as she could make it.

Donnie printed "HELP THE POOR" across the top of his poster in large letters. Then he put down his crayon and held it up for Mama to see.

"That's a nice poster, Donnie," said Mama.

"It will help you remember the canned goods," said Donnie, running to show it to Papa.

Mama nodded and turned back quickly to the stove.

When it was time to set the table, Mama asked Janet to put her things away when someone knocked at the door. It was Mrs. Cooper.

More Than Just a Ribbon

"I came to collect the rent for February," said the landlady, glancing around the room. When she saw Janet's poster, she said, "Very nice. You should meet my Sylvia."

Janet looked up at her.

"That's my daughter," said the landlady. "Sylvia's an artist, you see."

"A real one?" asked Janet, putting her crayons back in the box. She hadn't even known Mrs. Cooper had a daughter, and certainly not one who was an artist.

Mrs. Cooper sniffed. "Of course!" she said, taking the rent money from Mama. "Sylvia studied at the Art Institute. I'll have her stop by sometime."

"That would be nice," said Mama, smiling.

"Does she paint still lifes or what?" asked Janet, glad that she knew what a still life was. Mama looked surprised.

"Oh my, yes," said Mrs. Cooper, turning to leave. "She can paint anything—just as my father used to do."

Mrs. Cooper is starting to seem a little nice, thought

Janet. *And to think that her daughter's a real artist!* She wondered if Sylvia would look different from other people. Janet decided she'd probably wear a smock, and a beret on her head. Artists always wore berets. Rembrandt did, she remembered, and he was a famous artist. Her teacher in Columbia Heights had shown her a picture of Rembrandt in a book once. *Someday,* thought Janet, *when I'm rich and famous, I'm going to have a smock and a beret like Rembrandt's.*

After Mrs. Cooper left, Janet and Donnie were in the bathroom washing up for supper. Donnie said quietly, "I just heard Mama tell Papa that our money's almost gone."

Janet bit her lip and stared at the bubbles that were sliding down off her hands. "I know," she said, handing the soap to her brother.

"What's gonna happen?" said Donnie.

"I don't know, but Papa doesn't want to go on relief like some people. Me neither."

"What's relief?"

Janet shrugged. "The government gives you stuff—like clothes and food."

"So, what's wrong with that?"

"That's for poor people, Donnie. We're not poor!"

Donnie slipped the soap back into the dish. "Well, we might be, with no money," he said.

Janet just turned and left the room.

On Sunday afternoon, the Larsons were in the living room listening to the radio when they heard someone knock at the back door. Donnie jumped up and ran into the kitchen. He flung open the door.

Janet heard someone say, "Hi! Is your sister here?"

"Sure," said Donnie. It was Elaine.

Janet came up behind Donnie, and she pulled her friend inside. "What are you doing here?" said Janet, smiling weakly. What if Mrs. Cooper had seen Elaine coming through the backyard!

Elaine grinned. "I told you I knew where you lived."

"Oh, that's right," said Janet.

Mama called out, "Who's there, Janet?"

Janet brought Elaine into the living room and introduced her to her parents. "Elaine Carlson, eh?" said Papa, leaning forward. "You must be Sveedish."

"Oh yah!" giggled Elaine.

Papa smiled broadly. "It's nice to know there are some other Sveedes around here!"

Elaine told him that her family had come to Minneapolis a year ago from a small town up north. "My parents were born in Sweden, though," she said. Mama and Papa nodded approvingly. Then Elaine told them she went to the Swedish Lutheran church nearby.

"Oh, that's where we should go," said Mama. "It would be good to see our own people again. We've not yet found a church, and we've been lonesome here." She sighed.

Janet wondered how Mama could feel lonesome with nice people like the Polzacs living right next door.

Mama went with them into the kitchen and shut the door so Papa could hear his radio program. Then Mama told Elaine about Mrs. Cooper's rules. "The hardest one," she said quietly, "is that no children are supposed to visit us on Sundays."

Elaine clapped her hands up to her mouth. "Did she have those rules for the last family who lived here?"

"Probably," said Mama. "Why?"

Janet answered for Elaine, remembering what her new friend had told her on her first day at Howard School. "Elaine knew the people who used to live here, Mama," she said.

"The ones who got evicted?" her mother asked.

Elaine raised her eyebrows. "Evicted?"

"Oh, I'm sorry!" said Mama. "I thought you knew."

Elaine shook her head. "Doris Turner was a nice kid. . . . So was her whole family. Why would they get evicted?"

"The family was nice?" asked Janet, cracking a knuckle. "They weren't rowdy or anything?"

"I don't think so," said Elaine.

Janet could feel her stomach tightening.

"Well," said Mama, "maybe they couldn't pay their rent."

Elaine shrugged.

"I bet that was it," said Janet, glad she'd seen Mama give the rent money to Mrs. Cooper.

Elaine glanced up at the ceiling. "You think she saw me come in?" she asked.

Mama smiled. "I doubt it. You're so quiet." But she looked relieved when Elaine said she'd better leave.

"I know what!" said Janet. "Let's go and see if Eddie's home. Then we can play in his yard."

Eddie and Nicky were coming out of the Polzacs' back door when the girls came over. The boys looked at Elaine curiously until Janet introduced her. "We were just going to play with Butch and his cousins," said Eddie. "You two wanna come?"

Janet and Elaine smiled. "Sure!" they said.

Butch's three cousins made eight kids altogether, perfect for playing red rover and Captain-May-I?" When they got tired of those, they switched to hide-and-seek. Janet didn't want to tell the kids not to hide in her yard, but she finally did.

"Boy, I thought our landlady was strict," said one of Butch's cousins.

Janet nodded and didn't say any more. She wondered, though, how soon the kids would decide not to come around.

After school on Wednesday, Elaine came over to Janet's. They worked on their posters until it started getting dark. As she was putting on her coat, Elaine said, "I bet you win the contest, Janet."

"I bet you do," Janet said, wanting to be polite, but she was hoping Elaine was right. The letters on Elaine's poster were sort of crooked, and she really couldn't draw very well.

After the students brought their finished posters to school, a week dragged by before the winners were announced. Then all the fifth and sixth graders were brought together in the assembly room, where the best posters lay on a table up on the stage.

One by one, the principal, Mrs. Evans, held up the winning posters for everyone to see. A sixth-grade girl, who had drawn a pyramid of cans, got a yellow ribbon with the words "Honorable Mention" printed in gold. A fifth-grade boy got the third prize, a white ribbon, for his poster showing a wagonful of food. The red, second prize ribbon went to a sixth-grade boy who had drawn a thin hand reaching out for a can of soup. Everyone clapped each time a winning child hustled up to claim a ribbon.

Janet's eyes filled up. *I didn't get anything,* she thought. *All that work, and I didn't win.* If a sixth grader got second prize, they wouldn't pick . . .

All of a sudden she realized the principal had called her name. She looked around, and everyone was looking at her and clapping—even the boys. With her head down, but grinning, Janet made her way up to the stage, where Mrs. Evans was holding a blue ribbon.

"Janet Larson is new to Howard School," said Mrs. Evans, "and we're so glad that she had the courage to enter our contest."

Janet felt her cheeks burning.

"Janet's poster," continued the principal, "was very nicely drawn and is the most creative of them all!" She pointed. "Each can, as you can see, has a smile on it." She peered at Janet over her glasses. "The smiles must mean that the food we collect at Howard will bring happiness to others, right Janet?"

Janet nodded, but she didn't dare look out at the kids.

"One more thing," said Mrs. Evans, with a hand behind her back. "The first prize winner gets more than just a ribbon." She opened her hand, and Janet saw a Baby Ruth candy bar.

"For me?" asked Janet, holding her breath. She had never had a whole candy bar for herself, let alone a Baby Ruth bar.

"Yes, indeed, it's yours," said the principal, handing the candy to Janet.

Janet mumbled her thanks and returned to her seat as the children clapped again. She stared down at the red-and-white wrapper, wishing she could tear it open right there, but she'd have to wait until school was over. It wouldn't be polite to eat it in front of her classmates. She was glad, though, that Donnie was home with a cold that day. And that Elaine had to stay after school to help with a project. A true artist deserves a reward.

Only Temporary

Bang! Bang! Bang! Mrs. Cooper was pounding her cane on the floor again. Janet glanced at the ceiling and stuck out her tongue, but she did get up and turn down the radio. "Old fusspot!" she mumbled, as she threw herself back down into the overstuffed chair.

"Shhh," said Mama from the couch, jabbing her needle into the sock she was darning.

Janet crossed her arms. "I get so tired of her picking on us all the time."

"Maybe so," said Mama softly, "but we have to live with it for now." She looked over at Janet. "I thought you were getting to like Mrs. Cooper a little."

Janet shrugged. "Sometimes she acts nice."

"That's right," said Mama, "and don't forget how she gave you that nice drawing tablet."

"She said her daughter told her to. Her daughter sounds nicer than she is."

Mama shook her head. "Mrs. Cooper's daughter isn't renting out her house to a family of five, either." She cut off the thread and stuck the needle between her teeth.

Then Janet said, "It's not just because we're renting her house, Mama. Mrs. Cooper doesn't like the kids around here."

Mama removed the needle. "She likes Elaine," she said, shoving it into a pin cushion.

"Elaine doesn't live right around here," said Janet.

Mama smiled. "And she's quieter than the boys are," she said.

"But whenever Mrs. Cooper sees the boys her face freezes."

Mama laid the mended sock on its mate and started rolling the two together. "When I was your age," she said quietly, "I played with girls and dolls."

Janet rolled her eyes, but she wasn't ready to change the subject. "It's not just boys Mrs. Cooper doesn't like. She doesn't like the *kind* of people who live around here!"

"Keep your voice down," said her mother.

Papa and Donnie came into the room. Donnie plopped down on the couch next to his mother. Papa looked at Mama and then at Janet. "Vat's going on?" he asked.

Mama squinted as she threaded her needle again. "Oh, Janet's just wishing for the good old days."

"The good old days?" said Papa, slipping his arm around his daughter.

Janet pouted. "Remember how we used to have our whole house to ourselves? With no landlady?"

"Yah, I remember," said Papa wistfully, dropping his arm and moving over to the rocker. "Someday vee'll get another house," he said, easing himself down, "ven I get a job." He sighed.

Janet's eyes filled with tears. Another house seemed a million years away. Papa had looked for work almost every day since they'd moved to Minneapolis back in January. Here it was April, and there were still no jobs to be found.

"Well," said Donnie, pushing a small car along the rug, "at least now we get relief."

Donnie keeps track of everything people say, thought Janet, *even when he pretends he's not listening.*

Her little brother sat back on his heels. "Mama," he said, "tell me again about relief."

Mama laid her mending down on her lap. "Being on relief," she said, "means not having to worry about where your next meal is coming from." She looked sideways at her husband. "Relief means getting food and clothes from the government when you don't have the money to buy them."

Janet frowned and thought to herself, *being on relief means standing in long lines and having to wear clothes you hate.*

Papa went over and stared absently out the window. "Relief is no vay for a man to provide for his family," he said. "People vill think I'm a failure if they find out about it."

Mama shook her head. "Thousands of people are on relief, Karl, not just us. Besides," she said, tucking a spool back into her sewing basket, "this is only temporary. Things will get better soon, you'll see."

The next day a letter from Cambridge arrived in the morning mail. Papa read it aloud. The company Uncle Ed worked for had closed, and he, too, was out of a job. He wanted to know if Papa still wanted to look for work in another city. Janet listened and shuddered.

Two weeks later, after Papa had written back to Uncle Ed that he would work anywhere, the mailman left another letter from Columbia Heights. Papa tore it open and looked it over quickly. He called to Mama, "Anna! I can get a job!"

Mama came in from the bedroom. "Where?" she asked.

"In Chicago! Ed says they're hiring there now."

"Chicago?" Mama clasped her hands together. "Doing what?"

"Factory work. Yust a temporary job, but it's better than nothing." Uncle Ed had said he was leaving for Chicago on Sunday. Papa could ride with him, and they could stay with their brother, Sven, just as they had hoped.

Mama stood wringing her hands. "Karl," she said, "I'm not sure we can manage without you."

Papa went over and wrapped his arm around Mama. "It's only for a few veeks," he said. "And having some money vould make a big difference around here."

Mama nodded and blew her nose.

Donnie came into the kitchen. When he heard Papa's plans, he went over to him. "Who will tuck me in at night?" he asked. That had always been Papa's job.

Papa stroked Donnie's head and looked at Janet. "Your big sister vill help vith that," he said.

Janet smiled weakly, but when no one was looking she headed for the bathroom, where she stayed until she stopped crying.

On Sunday afternoon, Janet and Donnie stood by as Papa polished his worn shoes and packed his few clothes into a scuffed leather suitcase.

"Take some paper, so you can write us letters," said Janet.

"And three-cent stamps to mail them," said Donnie. "I'll send you a letter, too. I can write now, you know!"

Later, Papa took Janet by the chin and looked into her eyes. "Your mother is going to need your help more than ever vile I'm avay," he said.

Janet stared up at him and bit her lip.

Her father continued: "Remember Mrs. Cooper's rules! Please, Janet, be careful not to upset her."

Janet threw her arms around Papa and nodded against his soft shirt. She couldn't say anything because she was working her mouth to keep from crying.

A few moments later Papa dropped his arms. "Try to bring out the best in Mrs. Cooper, Janet, not the vurst," he said soberly.

Janet nodded. "I'll try, Papa," she said, but she wasn't sure whether the landlady had any "best" to bring out.

Donnie had been watching the street from the window in the front bedroom. "He's here!" he yelled.

All the Larsons threw on their coats and hustled outside as Uncle Ed's truck approached. Donnie ran ahead as Papa lugged the suitcase, and Mama followed with the lunch she had tucked into a paper sack. Janet grabbed Patty's hand and helped her slowly down the concrete steps to the street.

A-oogah! A-oogah! went the horn. Uncle Ed pulled up to the curb and sat grinning behind the large steering wheel as Donnie jumped up on the running board. The engine made the whole truck vibrate, and it was hard to hear each other over the noise. Everyone crowded around.

"All aboard for Chicago! Seats left for workers only!" yelled Uncle Ed, winking from the empty truck.

Papa gave everyone a last hug and climbed up into the broad front seat next to his brother. Mama leaned toward the open window and yelled something in Swedish.

They all laughed, and the truck started to pull away from the curb. Suddenly, though, the engine stopped dead.

Uncle Ed jumped out, ran around to the front, and started cranking the engine. Everyone watched solemnly as Ed cranked and cranked. Soon the engine sputtered and coughed, and the truck started shaking again. Uncle Ed got back into the driver's seat.

"Off vee go!" he shouted. Both men threw kisses, everyone waved, and the truck started rolling down Washington Street. Janet and Donnie kept waving until it disappeared around a corner.

As they started back up the walk, Janet noticed that green grass was beginning to peek through the crusted snow at the edges of the concrete and bright splotches of color were sprouting next to the fence. "Look!" she said, pointing. "Flowers!"

"Crocuses," said Mama. "Well, it's almost May after all." The children ran across the front yard to get a closer look at the yellow and purple blossoms. "Back on the side-walk!" said Mama, shaking her head. "Remember the rules!"

Janet glanced up at Mrs. Cooper's front window. The lace curtain dropped quickly into place, but not before she caught a glimpse of the landlady frowning at them through the glass.

Chapter 1

1934

On Relief

Janet sat on the bed, watching sullenly as her mother lifted her faded blue cloche from a round box and set it on her head. Close-fitting hats like that were out of style now, but it was the only one Mama had, and no woman—even in the Depression—would think of going out without her head covered.

"Of course you have to go with us," said Mama, moving over to the dresser. "You know I can't get anything done at relief headquarters unless you're there to keep an eye on Donnie and Patty." She squinted into the mirror as she jabbed a long, pearl-headed pin into the headband.

"I hate that place," whined Janet, zipping up Patty's jacket. "It's full of yelling kids."

Mama nodded. "And that's exactly why I need you there. People will see that Swedish children, at least, know how to behave!"

"How will they know we're Swedish?" asked Donnie.

"Our last name is on the order," said Mama.

Relief orders were printed on blue tissue paper, and families on relief got four different kinds: for fuel, rent, food, and clothes. They could use food orders in any grocery store, but they had to go to headquarters to get clothes.

"I wish Papa could go with us," said Donnie, twisting a lock of hair. Papa and Uncle Ed had been in Chicago for a week, but he'd written that the job there lasted only two days. They were going to stay awhile, though, and keep looking for something else.

Mama gave Donnie a hug. "Your papa will be back as soon as he can," she said, "but in the meantime, we can get some clothes by ourselves—if we all help."

Just as they were ready to leave, though, someone knocked at the door. It was Mrs. Cooper, and a young woman was with her. She was slim and dark-haired, and her coat had fur around the collar.

"Won't you come in?" said Mama, standing aside.

The two women entered. Mrs. Cooper looked at Mama's hat. "I see you're going out," she said, hesitating.

"Yes, but we can wait a bit," said Mama. Janet saw her mother glance at the clock. "Come and sit down."

"No, no," said the landlady, "we can't stay anyway." She gestured toward the young woman. "I just wanted you to meet my daughter, Sylvia," she said. "The artist," she added proudly.

Janet stared at her. Sylvia's coat was open, and she had on a dress—no smock and no beret.

"Well, Janet," said Sylvia, smiling. She was holding a paper bag. "Mother told me you won a poster contest."

Janet nodded.

"We're so proud of her!" said Mama, hoisting Patty to her hip.

Sylvia reached into the bag. "I thought maybe you could use these." She held out a watercolor paint box. "I don't need them anymore."

"For me?" asked Janet, wide-eyed.

Mrs. Cooper beamed. "Sylvia's painting with oils these days."

Janet opened the shiny black metal box. Inside were two long rows of bright-colored paint squares, hardly used. Between the paints lay two brushes, a thick one and a skinny one. She'd never seen a paint box with so many different shades of paint. Janet swallowed hard. "Thank you!" she said. "Thank you ever so much! These are wonderful."

"Well, I hope you'll enjoy them," said Sylvia, turning to leave. "Keep up the good work!"

"I will!" Janet promised, still gazing at the paints.

When they were gone, Mama said to Janet, "There! See how nice Mrs. Cooper can be?"

Janet had to agree, but she said, "Maybe she learned that from her daughter!"

A few minutes later, as Mama hustled the children out the back door, Janet said, "I wish I could stay home and paint."

Mama smiled. "The sooner we go, the sooner we'll be back, and then you can paint to your heart's content!" As they headed toward the shed, she added, "You kids can take turns pulling Patty in the wagon."

As Janet turned to pull the Radio Flyer up the walk to the old school building that served as relief headquarters, she saw Joey, from her class, across the street. Janet kept her head down and turned in the other direction, hoping he wouldn't see her and realize where she was going.

"What are you looking at?" Donnie called out from behind.

"Nothing. My neck hurts," said Janet.

"Then I'll help pull the wagon up the steps," said her little brother.

Inside, dozens of people had already lined up in the gymnasium to get their clothes orders filled. Mama left the children in the dimly lit hallway and joined the end of the line.

Janet helped Donnie get started with the wagon so that he could pull Patty up and down the length of the long hallway. Patty sat clutching her ragged security blanket with one hand and the side of the Radio Flyer with the other, staring at people as she passed.

Janet sat down on a wooden bench near the end of the hall. She pulled her coat collar up and kept her head down, hoping no one from school was around. After a while someone came over and sat down next to her. From the corner of her eyes, Janet could see a that it was a woman in a brown coat. She sat hunched forward, squeezing her hands. She started talking. "I get so tired of waiting wherever I go," she said.

Janet turned and looked at her face. The woman's limp, gray hair fell around the worn collar of her coat, and there was a gaping hole where one of her front teeth should have been. "Wait in the clinic," said the woman, "wait for the orders—wait, wait, wait. Isn't it awful being poor?"

"Oh, we're not poor," said Janet.

"You're on relief, aren't you?"

"Yes, but . . ."

"Then you're poor, honey," said the woman, but Janet just tossed her head and looked away.

Donnie and Patty came by again, waving at Janet.

"That your little brother and sister?" asked the woman, after they had passed.

chapter seven

"Uh-huh," said Janet.

"Such pretty blond hair! Bet your folks are Scandinavian."

Janet nodded. "Swedish," she replied. No one ever said Janet's brown hair was pretty.

"Swedish. That's nice."

Janet wasn't sure what was so nice about just being Swedish. She had seen some drunk people outside a bar on Central Avenue, and some of them were speaking Swedish, she could tell.

Donnie returned, holding Patty by the hand and pulling an empty wagon. "She wet her pants," he said.

Great, thought Janet, *now I get to clean up the puddle the nice little Swedish girl made in the Radio Flyer.*

Later, they went back down to the gym, and Mama was at the head of the line. She took Patty from Janet and handed the clothes order to an unsmiling woman at the desk. The woman banged the paper with a stamp. "Clothes first and then shoes," she snapped, reaching for the next person's order.

Janet looked at the rows of cotton dresses that sagged on their hangers. They were alike except for the fabrics: half were blue-and-white checked, and the others were pink-and-green flowered. Their sizes were printed on green paper and pinned on with safety pins.

Mama and Janet and Patty each got two dresses. Donnie got shirts and short pants, and everyone got pajamas, all made of the same speckled fabric.

"Hold still," said Mama, checking carefully to be sure everything fit. The first clothes they had gotten with relief orders had been much too large, and Mama had spent hours at the sewing machine taking them in. Janet was glad her mother could sew well. She could add a collar or change some buttons, and then maybe no one would know where the clothes had come from.

Shoes, though, could not be changed, and when Janet saw what they gave her, she thought they had made a mistake. The shoes were oxfords—stiff and brown—and they laced up like Papa's shoes. Janet took them back to the man in charge. "I think I got the wrong pair," she told him, trying to stay calm.

He grabbed one of the shoes and looked inside. His fat cigar dropped ashes as he spoke. "They're size 3. That your size?"

Janet nodded soberly.

"Then move along," said the man. "We got no choices and lotsa people waiting."

Janet could feel her throat tighten. She turned to Mama. "These aren't kids' shoes," she said softly, pleading with her eyes.

Mama shifted Patty in her arms. "It's all they have, dear."

As they worked their way back through the crowd, Janet kept her eyes down on the scuffed gym floor with its traces of red and black paint, trying to hide her tears. Back out in the hallway she stopped. "Mama," she said, shaking her head, "I can't wear these shoes anywhere!"

Mama fumbled in her purse for a handkerchief and handed it to Janet. She didn't say anything, but Janet saw tears in her eyes, too.

Janet pretended to be very busy with the empty wagon as they left the old school building. As the wheels clunked down the steps, she vowed to herself: Never will I wear those shoes! Not ever!

When they got back out on the sidewalk, Mama tucked Patty and the clothes bags firmly into the wagon, picked up the handle, and started for home. She walked very fast.

Donnie lagged behind and slipped his hand into Janet's. "When Papa gets a job," he said, "we can go to a real shoe store again. Then everything will be just like it used to be."

Janet nodded, but she didn't believe it. Nothing was like it used to be, and it never would be.

They were about halfway home when Janet noticed someone coming up from behind them. It was Skinny Slominski and his mother, and they were pulling a wagon, too.

"Hey, Janet!" yelled Skinny. "Wait up!"

The Larsons stopped. In a few moments the Slominskis were on the sidewalk right next to them. It was the first time Janet had been up close to Mrs. Slominski, who smiled broadly at seeing her neighbors. Her straight dark bangs peeked out from the kerchief she wore around her head. She quickly introduced herself, and Mama did the same, smiling weakly in return.

Mrs. Slominski looked down at the Larsons' loaded wagon. "I see you've been 'shopping,' too," she laughed.

Something in her voice made Mama stiffen. "This is only temporary," Mama said politely. "My husband is between jobs right now."

"Right!" said Mrs. Slominski, still smiling. "Well, I hear President Roosevelt has a plan to get everyone working again."

Mama nodded and started pulling the wagon. Janet fell into step alongside Skinny.

"Didya get some new clothes?" he asked.

"If you can call them that," mumbled Janet.

"It's better than nothin'."

Janet wasn't so sure. Then she heard Mrs. Slominski behind her saying, "Well, at least with rent orders we don't have to worry anymore about getting evicted."

The word "evicted" made Janet shudder. Her family needed more than just rent orders with mean old Mrs. Cooper around.

Chapter 5

1934

Remember Who You Are

Two weeks had passed, and a spring rain was pounding Minneapolis as Janet and Donnie trudged to Sunday School. After Elaine's first visit, back in February, the Larsons had started attending the Swedish Lutheran church she had told them about. Mama and Papa liked the people they met there, and they made sure that Janet and Donnie were in Sunday School every week. Elaine, of course, was there, and so were some other kids from her class in school.

As they walked along, Janet tried to remember to tilt Papa's old black umbrella so it covered both herself and her brother. When she forgot, Donnie would yank on the handle, sending a reminding shower across her back.

Water streamed across the sidewalks in rivulets and up through the holes in Janet's shoes. "My toes are squishing!" she squealed, stepping carefully to avoid the deeper puddles.

"I thought you fixed your shoes," said Donnie. The

night before, he had watched Janet cut out cardboard soles to line them.

"They were okay for a while," she said.

Donnie tugged at the umbrella again. "Bet you wish you'd worn your new shoes."

"Nope!" said Janet. "So what if my feet get wet. I'm never gonna wear those icky brown shoes. Besides, when summer comes, I'm going barefoot!"

"To Sunday School?"

Janet tossed her head. "Well, maybe I just won't go in the summertime," she snorted.

Even though they had hurried through the rain, the children arrived at the brick church with its tall steeple just as the Sunday School superintendent was closing the heavy wooden door. "Yust in the nick of time!" said Mr. Carlson, clapping Donnie on the shoulder. He led the way down the broad oak staircase to the basement and toward a muffled din behind a pair of doors. He pushed through one of them, and Janet and Donnie followed.

The fellowship hall was buzzing, as usual, before the opening exercises. Dozens of boys, squirming in neckties and woolen knickers, sought each other out and started shoving and snickering. But at the sound of "Onward, Christian Soldiers," pounded out on the piano by Mrs. Dahlgren, the minister's wife, everyone raced to the chairs. The older boys grabbed the front row seats, leaving the younger ones to file in behind them. The girls were content to sit farther back, where they could keep an eye on their brothers and report back to their mothers. Janet found Elaine, and they sat next to each other, as they always did. Janet sometimes wished she could sit up front with the boys, but Elaine never wanted to.

"Today," said Mr. Carlson, from the platform, "vee

vill be thinking about children in far-avay Africa. How many of you know vhere Africa is?"

Most of the older children raised their hands. Donnie looked back at Janet and then raised his, too.

"Do you know," continued Mr. Carlson, "that there are children in Africa who have never heard of Yee-sus?" Janet had never heard anyone say "Jesus" like Mr. Carlson did.

The children nodded in response to the superintendent's question. Janet knew what was coming next.

"Vell, then, how vill they hear about Yee-sus?" he asked. Mr. Carlson's bald head was as shiny as his eyeglasses. He squinted at the fresh-scrubbed faces and waited.

A little girl in the back raised her hand. "We can help?" she asked timidly.

"Yes!" boomed Mr. Carlson. "And how can vee help?"

"With our pennies," she replied, and several others chimed in with her, not bothering to raise their hands.

With that, Mrs. Dahlgren struck some notes on the piano, a song that everyone knew: "Hear Our Pennies Dropping."

Almost on cue, the children moved out to the aisle and filed toward the platform, where a large glass jar stood on a small table. Mrs. Dahlgren beamed and kept playing, and the children chanted as they marched.

> Hear our pennies dropping, see them as they fall;
> Every one for Jesus, He will get them all . . .

Janet followed Elaine and the rest of the girls who joined a long line that kept moving toward the platform. She could still feel how soaked her socks were.

Elaine turned to say something to Janet, but Janet had stopped briefly, trying to loosen her pennies from her handkerchief. Somehow Mama managed to save out six pennies for Sunday School every single week—three for Janet and three for Donnie. Lucky Donnie could carry his in a pants pocket, but Janet's were always tied into a knot in her handkerchief. Mama would pin the handkerchief to Janet's waist so that the money didn't get lost.

Janet moved along, trying to catch up with Elaine while she fumbled with the lumpy knot. To her relief, it finally loosened just in time for her to slip her pennies into the jar. Janet had wondered at first how the money could get to Jesus up in heaven, but Mr. Carlson had said it would, and that was enough for her.

Later, Mrs. Swanson, Janet's teacher, had the class pull their chairs into a circle during lesson time so that they faced each other. "Our story for today," she said, "is about Jesus and the children." Mrs. Swanson held a large picture on her lap, turned so that the class could see it as she talked. It showed Jesus and His disciples standing together, but there weren't any children in the picture. "Some children wanted to see Jesus," the teacher continued, "but His helpers, the disciples, tried to send the children away. 'Don't bother Jesus,' said the men, moving the children back toward their mothers. 'Can't you see He's busy?' When Jesus saw what was happening, though, He told the men to bring the little children back to Him, because He wanted to hug them."

Then Mrs. Swanson held up another picture, one of Jesus surrounded by children of all sizes and colors. There were children with white faces, and black, brown, and yellow faces. Some stood next to Jesus, and some sat at His feet. And He held a little black boy on His lap.

"Did they have names like ours?" asked Ruth Ann Engstrom.

Mrs. Swanson smiled. "We don't know what they were," she replied. "They probably had many different names, just as we do today," she added.

Like Larson and Polzac and Butowsky, thought Janet. Jesus wouldn't keep anyone out of His yard, if He had one. She wondered if Mrs. Cooper had ever heard that story.

With everyone facing each other in the circle, Janet noticed that Elaine was wearing brown oxfords exactly like the ones she'd gotten at relief headquarters. They had the same laces and everything. Why would Elaine pick out dumb shoes like that from a shoe store? she wondered.

Donnie saw the shoes, too, as Janet and her friends stood around together after class. "Look," said Donnie, pointing. "Her shoes are just like yours!"

Janet narrowed her eyes. Why couldn't Donnie keep his mouth shut?

"What did you say?" asked Elaine.

Before Janet could stop him, Donnie said, louder, "Janet has shoes just like yours at home, but she won't wear them anywhere."

Janet felt like punching Donnie.

Elaine's face turned red. "That's what I used to say, too," she said softly. "But then my old ones got too tight."

Janet bit her lip. So Elaine had gotten her shoes with relief orders, just as she had! *I should have known,* she thought. She put her arm around Elaine and whispered, "I'm going to wear my brown shoes, then, too."

When they got home, Janet helped Mama set the table for dinner. As usual on Sundays, they put on a real tablecloth, instead of the oilcloth they used all week, and they got out the good china and glassware.

"Why do we always have to use the good stuff on Sundays?" asked Janet, placing a fork next to each plate. "Papa's not here. Why bother?"

Mama filled a glass with milk. "So we will remember who we are," she said, setting it down on the table. "We are the Larsons, and we are no different than before."

"Before Papa lost his store?"

Mama nodded. "Remember," she said, "this is only temporary. Times will get better."

Janet wished she could be as sure as Mama was.

When dinner was ready and everyone was at the table, Janet looked at Papa's empty chair and her eyes filled up. He had been gone only three weeks, but it seemed like a year.

Without Papa there to say grace, Mama bowed her head and started the Swedish prayer they always prayed on Sundays. Janet and Donnie joined in:

> *I Jesu namn till bords vi gå*
> *Välsigna Gud den mat vi få.*
> (In Jesus' name we take our seat;
> Father, bless the food we eat.)

Donnie unfolded his napkin. "Mama, can God speak Swedish?" he said.

Mama placed some small pieces of meat loaf on Patty's plate. "What?" she asked. Then she added quickly, "Of course He can."

"Can He speak American, too?"

"English, Donnie," said Janet, helping herself to a thin slice of meat loaf.

"Well, can He?"

Mama hesitated a moment, and then she said, "God

understands every language, Donnie."

Janet looked down at her plate and snickered, but her brother was determined.

"Well, how come we have to pray in Swedish, then?" he asked.

Mama stopped and looked at Donnie. "We don't. I just like for you to use the prayer I learned when I was a little girl."

Donnie nodded. "Maybe it works better if you send it both ways, huh?"

"Can't hurt to try," said Mama, but her smile faded quickly.

Janet was flattening her potatoes with her fork. She paused and looked at Mama. "If God can understand everything," she said, "how come He doesn't make the Depression go away?"

"Humph!" said Mama. "I guess everyone wishes He'd do that!"

"But why doesn't He?"

Mama sat quietly for a moment. "Well," she said, "I think God expects us to do everything we can for ourselves first of all."

Janet thought about Papa in Chicago. "Like keep looking for a job?"

Mama smiled. "Right."

"And give food to the poor!" said Donnie.

"Sure," said Mama, looking off into the distance.

Janet knitted her brow. "And after that, then what?"

Mama took a deep breath. "My goodness," she said, "you certainly are full of questions today!"

Janet grinned.

Mama continued, but Janet had the feeling she was almost talking to herself. "I don't know just how it's going to happen," she said, "but somehow God's going to help someone to figure out how to make things better in our country." Then she added, "And give us the courage to manage until they are!"

Janet smiled at Mama and silently asked God for the courage to wear her awful brown shoes. And to help her find out if Mrs. Cooper really did have a "best" side. She kept squashing her potato until finally Mama raised an eyebrow.

Chapter 9

1934

Trouble

By the time Janet had helped put away the dinner dishes, the sun was streaming through the kitchen windows. Everything outside looked washed and glistening.

Mama went out to put the empty milk bottles on the back porch. When she came back she asked, "How would you like to go down to see Mrs. Benson's new baby? It's only two o'clock, so we have time for a nice walk in this good weather."

"Do we have to go *now?*" asked Janet.

"Soon as we can get ready."

"But I was going to play bounce-out. Do I have to go?"

Mama shrugged. "I suppose I can take just Donnie and Patty." She started to get out her hat. "Promise you'll stay in the alley."

"That's the only place you can play bounce-out around here, Mama," said Janet.

"You know what I mean. No kids in the yard."

Janet wrinkled up her nose. "I know."

A few minutes later Mama was heading up the street with Donnie and Patty in the wagon. Janet circled the house and crossed the yard toward the alley.

The alley divided the city block into halves and held them together like a concrete zipper. Every morning the milkman and the iceman drove from one end to the other to deliver bottles of milk or blocks of ice at their customers' back doors. And because few families could afford cars anymore, the alley was a safe place to play Captain-May-I?, kick-the-can, and bounce-out.

Eddie and Nicky were waiting when Janet came running up. "Anyone else playing?" she asked.

"Butch, whenever he gets here," said Eddie, setting an empty tin can down in the center of the concrete. Eddie was a champion at kick-the-can.

"I thought we were playing bounce-out," said Janet, crossing her arms.

"I'm just practicing," said Eddie, swinging hard with his right foot. The can sailed through the air and landed far up the alley, clanging loudly and rattling continuously as it rolled back down toward the children.

"Good shot, Eddie!" called Nicky, grabbing the can and setting it upright again. "My turn," he said, taking aim. There was another loud clang, followed by more rattling.

The boys kept this up until Butch arrived, trailed by Sandra, his little sister. Sandra was eight, and she was usually off playing with Nicky's sister.

"No dolls today?" Janet teased when Sandra came up. Janet had always thought dolls were dumb.

Sandra shook her head. "Mary Ann's not home," she said. Then she asked Nicky, "Can I play?"

Nicky rolled his eyes. "You gotta know how," he

said, watching as Butch stepped up for a turn at kicking.

Sandra put her hands on her hips. "I played once."

"She can be a fielder," said Eddie. Sandra grinned and headed to where Eddie had pointed.

The game began, and soon everyone was alternately cheering or booing as they took turns fielding and batting, and one batter after the other either made hits or got "bounced out." After the rain earlier, the players were full of energy—and louder than usual.

Before long, five of the Slominski kids from up the alley came to join them. Mama called the Slominskis "stair steps," because they were all only a year apart—each just an inch or two taller or shorter than the next in age. The first time Janet had played at their house, she'd returned home breathless. "Mama," she'd said, "the Slominskis have seven kids! All my age or younger."

Mama didn't even look up from the ironing board. "I wonder where they put them all," she said quietly.

"And guess what, Mama!" Janet had said, her eyes widening. "They've got twin babies!"

Mama rubbed the iron back and forth across a pillowcase, and all she said was, "Really?" But Janet still envied the Slominskis.

With five more players, the game got rowdier—and noisier—than ever. When Janet thought about it later, she wished they'd stopped playing when Mrs. Butowski called Butch and Sandra in to dinner. They'd been at it a long time, and their shadows stretched far down the alley. Janet knew her mother would call her in as soon as she came home, but she wasn't back yet. She shivered, buttoned up her sweater, and stepped up for her turn as catcher.

Nicky stood in front of her, swinging the bat back and forth over the hunk of cardboard that served as home plate, just like Babe Ruth in the newsreels. Skinny Slominski was pitching, and in no time he sent the ball spinning toward Nicky. Nicky swung hard, the ball disappeared into the twilight, and only a loud bang told them where it landed: on the tin roof under Mrs. Cooper's window.

Like a shot, Skinny dashed into Janet's yard.

"No!" called Janet, clapping her hands to her face.

The upstairs window flew open, and the ballplayers froze in their tracks. "You nearly broke my window, young man!" yelled Mrs. Cooper. "And what are you doing in my flowers?"

Janet held her breath as Skinny fished around frantically in the iris bed beneath the landlady's window. "Sorry! I'm just gettin' the ball," he said. He found it and tucked it under his arm, then spun around and headed back to the alley.

Mrs. Cooper shook her finger. "You stay out of this yard!" She banged the window shut.

Back in the alley, Skinny said, "Wow, is she always like that?"

Janet shrugged. "We're just not supposed to play in her yard." She tried to sound calm, but she could feel her heart pounding.

"Well, he didn't break nothin'," said Skinny's brother, Wally, pulling off his cap and scratching his head.

"I know," said Janet. She looked over at Skinny. "It's not your fault. She's just got these dumb rules we have to follow, or we might get evicted."

"Evicted? You mean you'd get thrown out just for that?" said Skinny. "Wow, we'd better scram!"

One by one, everyone left but Eddie and Nicky. Janet bit her lip and kicked the cardboard base. Eddie picked up his ball and bat. "Next time we'll play farther up the alley," he said. "Then Old Lady Cooper won't bother us."

Janet sniffed. "If anyone ever wants to play again, you mean," she said. She turned to go home.

"We'll play again," said Nicky, following her. "We just don't want to get you in trouble, that's all."

Eddie stopped. "You're not, are you, Janet?"

"What, in trouble with Mrs. Cooper?" said Janet, flipping her hair back. "Why should I be? We didn't break anything."

"I know, but she sure was mad."

"It's okay." Janet tossed her head and started up her driveway, but she was glad Mama wasn't home. At the fence that separated her yard from Eddie's, she looked up at him with envy. "You're lucky you don't have a landlady at your house."

Eddie smiled. "We do, sort of. She's my mother."

"Your mother?"

"My folks own our house, and we rent the upstairs out to someone else."

"Oh." Janet stopped and cocked her head. "Hey, I've got it!" she said. "Maybe we could swap landladies!"

Just then something small darted across the driveway and disappeared under a clump of dandelions near the corner of the shed. "What was that?" asked Janet.

"Whatever it is, it's trapped back there," said Nicky. He slowly pushed back the jagged leaves, and they leaned in for a look.

"It's a SNAKE!" said Janet.

Eddie nodded. "Looks like a baby garter."

"How do you know?"

"See those stripes on its back? That's how you can tell."

"Then it's not poisonous or anything," said Janet,

kneeling down so she could see it better.

"No, it won't hurt you," said Eddie.

"Probably scared to death," said Nicky.

"Poor thing!" said Janet. "Maybe we could take it home!"

Eddie grinned. "Not me! My mom says one mouse is more than enough."

"Bet I could keep it," said Janet eagerly. A snake was better than no pet at all. "Think we could get it into my fishbowl?"

By the time her mother came home, Janet's slinky visitor lay curled up in her fishbowl—on the kitchen table. Mama didn't see it right away, and she had just started to tell Janet something when Donnie interrupted them. "What's that?" he asked, as soon as he came into the room and saw the fishbowl.

Mama followed his eyes. "Oh, no! Not a snake!" she said.

"It's okay, Mama," said Janet. "It can't get out." Eddie had laid a piece of wire screening over the top and held it in place with a stone.

Donnie climbed up on a chair to get closer. "What are you gonna feed it?"

"Bugs."

Mama scowled. "And just where are you going to get them?" she asked.

"There're lots of bugs in the shed," said Janet. "Ants and spiders . . . and the spiders catch flies with their webs. I've seen them."

Donnie looked more and more interested. "I'll help you catch them!" he said. "We can put them in a jar."

Mama finally agreed that Janet could keep the snake for a few days provided she take it into the shed. "And don't you dare let that thing get loose," said Mama, shaking her head as she started getting things out for supper.

Janet carried the bowl carefully into the musty, low-ceilinged shed and set it on a shelf near the window. Then she ran back into the house for something to hold drinking water. When she returned, Donnie was pulling a struggling fly from a spider web. He flipped it down next to the snake. "First meal in his new home!" said Donnie, grinning.

"It's a girl snake, not a boy," said Janet, slowly lowering a jar lid brimming with water down into the bowl.

"How do you know it's a girl?" said Donnie.

Janet pulled her hand back out. "It just is," she said. "And I'm going to call her Samantha."

"That's a dumb name for a snake." Donnie pinched at another fly.

"So, how many snakes have *you* named?" said Janet, watching as her brother dropped a second fly into the bowl. Then they went outside and got some leaves and sticks so that Samantha would feel at home.

When the children were both satisfied that the snake would be all right for the night, they returned to the kitchen. Mama had given Patty her supper, and she was struggling to wipe the food from Patty's chin. "I started to tell you," said Mama, scrubbing with the washcloth, "I might get a job!"

"A job?" said Janet. Mothers didn't work, fathers did. And besides, if Papa couldn't find a job, how could Mama? "How can you do that?" asked Janet.

"I can work right here at home with my sewing machine!" Mama continued. She lifted Patty from her high chair and set her down on the floor. "I heard this afternoon that they need someone to make costumes for a Swedish festival over in South Minneapolis. You remember Alice

Peterson? Well, I heard she needs a dozen costumes made, and she'll pay a dollar for each one! Just think! A whole dollar!" Mama almost danced around the room. Then she added quickly, "I have to let her know right away or I might miss out. Watch the kids for a few minutes, will you?" She pulled her coat from its hook. "I'm going down to the drugstore to call Alice."

Janet watched as her mother slipped into her coat. "Mama," she said, "Mrs. Polzac said we can use their telephone anytime we need to."

"That's nice, dear, but I'd do that only in an emergency. Besides, the drugstore is not far. I'll be gone only a minute." Mama closed the door firmly as she hurried off.

Janet followed Patty into the living room. Donnie was sitting on the rug, cutting paper snakes out of newspaper. Janet sat on the rug and leaned back against the couch. She watched as Patty grabbed Donnie's scraps and sat tearing them into little pieces. A few minutes later, someone knocked on the door.

Donnie jumped up and opened it. It was Mrs. Cooper.

Bad News and Good

The landlady stood so close to the open doorway that Janet caught her breath. "Is your mother here?" she demanded.

"Not right now," said Janet, "but she'll be back soon." She tried to smile at Mrs. Cooper, but the echo of the slamming window still hung between them.

Donnie nudged closer to Janet. Patty tried to push past both of them and out into the hallway, but Janet grabbed her and hoisted her up on her hip.

"You and your Polack friends gave me quite a fright this afternoon," said the landlady, crossing her arms.

Janet's eyes narrowed.

"That ball could have broken my window."

"I know. We'll be more careful next time."

Mrs. Cooper stiffened. "Next time?"

"Next time we play, I mean."

"Not in my yard!"

"We weren't playing in your yard. The ball—"

"Just keep that ball out of my yard."

Janet fought to keep from saying any more. "Yes, Mrs. Cooper."

The woman started for the stairs as Mama burst in the front door. She stopped when she saw Mrs. Cooper. "Is something wrong?" she asked.

Janet would have given anything to turn around and run at that point. Instead she lowered her eyes and waited while the landlady, standing rigidly, told Mama how noisy her friends had been and how the ball had nearly broken her window. Janet could feel her heart pounding, hearing the landlady's version.

Mama turned angrily to Janet. "Were you playing in the yard?"

Janet shook her head vigorously. "No, Mama. We were in the alley."

Mrs. Cooper snorted, "Close enough to hit my window!"

"But we weren't in the yard!"

"Nevertheless, that ball could have broken my window! It's a miracle it didn't. If that glass had—"

Mama said calmly, "But the ball didn't hit the window, Mrs. Cooper. And I'm sure the children were sorry it happened."

Janet nodded as she set Patty down. She wanted to hug Mama right then and there.

Mrs. Cooper was not easily silenced. "I can see, Mrs. Larson, that we're just going to have further trouble if those young . . ." She looked over at Janet, whose eyes were flashing now with anger. ". . . if those young ruffians don't stay out of the yard and away from my house. Do you understand?"

This time it was Mama's eyes that were flashing.

"Yes, Mrs. Cooper," she said, "we understand, all right. And now, I hope you'll excuse us." She spun around, pushed the children back through the living room door, and shut it firmly behind them. Then she took Janet by the shoulders, whispering gruffly, "Your father told you not to anger that woman, and now look what you've done!"

Janet shrugged free and ran to her room, burying her face in her pillow as the sobs broke out. After a long while her mother came in and sat down next to her. Mama quietly stroked Janet's back.

Janet raised her head. Donnie and Patty were in the doorway, watching.

"She's an old witch," sobbed Janet.

"Shush! Keep your voice down! Do you want to tell me now exactly what happened?"

Janet sat cross-legged on the bed and told her mother her version of the ball game. Mama agreed that Mrs. Cooper's reaction was unfair.

"Unfair? It was mean!" said Janet.

"Mean, mean," mimicked Patty, climbing up on Mama's lap.

"You're right, Janet," said Mama. "It was mean of her." She sighed and sat holding Patty until she wriggled free and toddled back to Donnie. Mama continued, "The worst of it is, Jan, there's absolutely nothing we can do about it."

"The worst of it is she calls my friends Polacks!"

Mama looked puzzled.

"My teacher said Polack is a bad word."

"Well, you know what she means: Polish."

"Well then, why doesn't she say that?"

"Because everybody knows . . ."

"Why call them anything? Why not just call them

kids?" Janet's eyes filled up again. "I wish we were back in Columbia Heights!" she said. "Everybody there was nice!"

"Not everybody," said Mama. "There are people like Mrs. Cooper everywhere. You had just never met any before."

"Well, I wish I'd never met *her!*"

Mama sat silently for a moment. Finally she said, "Well, I don't have any magic wands. We're just going to have to make the best of it until we can afford another place to live." She smiled. "At least you're old enough to go elsewhere and visit your friends."

Janet wasn't ready to look at the bright side of it. She frowned and wiped her tears on her sleeve. "I wish Papa were here," she grumbled.

"It's just as well he wasn't here this afternoon," said Mama, heading for the kitchen. But when Janet joined her a few minutes later, Mama was looking wistfully out the window. "In his last letter Papa sounded as if he might have to give up on job hunting in Chicago. It's no better there than it is here." Then she turned to Janet and brightened. "Well, at least I got the job."

"You did?"

"Yep! Promised Alice I'd have a dozen Swedish costumes ready by June twelfth. That's three weeks from now."

As the evening wore on, Mama told Janet that the costumes were to look authentic—white blouses and shirts, colorful skirts and pants, lots of braid and rickrack trimming, and even red suspenders for the men. "It's a good thing I have Papa's old pictures to go by," said Mama. She looked over at Janet. "It's going to take a lot of cooperation to get everything done on time."

"I know," said Janet. *That means I get stuck with the kids*, she thought.

As Mama was putting Patty to bed, Janet started the dishes. Their sink was very small, so they usually washed dishes on the kitchen table. Janet spread clean towels over the oilcloth and set down two dishpans. As she did, she thought about Papa. She missed him so much. *Why did he have to leave us in this stupid house?* she thought. *Why couldn't Papa's store have stayed open? Then we could have stayed in Columbia Heights.*

The teakettle, sitting on the back of the stove, was beginning to whistle when Mama came back into the kitchen.

"Mama," asked Janet, "whose fault is it?"

"Whose fault is what?" asked Mama, reaching for a pot holder.

"Who made Papa's store close?"

Mama pushed her hair out of her eyes and lifted the whistling teakettle. "Nobody made it close, Janet. It had to be done, that's all. There were just too many bills—too many bills." She shook her head and poured steaming water into the pans. She refilled the teakettle and added some cold water to the dishpans.

Janet thought for a minute and asked, "But whose fault was it that Papa couldn't pay the bills?"

"It wasn't any one person's fault," said Mama, setting glasses down into the sudsy water.

"Well, someone should have made the people pay Papa the money they owed him. Then he could have kept his store and we wouldn't have had to move."

"You can't make people pay bills when they don't have any money and they can't get work," said Mama, quickly moving the glasses into the rinse water. "That's what's so terrible about the Depression. It just keeps spreading and spreading." One by one, Mama lifted the glasses and set them on a towel to drain.

Janet wiped the dishes slowly and set them in the cupboard, but thoughts about Mrs. Cooper kept racing through her head. *We ought to get even with that old witch!* she thought, not noticing that her mother had said something to her.

"Did you hear me?" asked Mama.

"What?"

"I said I'm going to need your help when I do the sewing," said Mama.

"I know." *Revenge,* thought Janet. *That's what's I want: revenge!*

"I have an appointment with Mrs. Peterson tomorrow at four. You'll have to watch the children for me as soon as you get home from school."

"Okay."

"Remember, I've got only three weeks."

"Uh-huh," said Janet. Maybe Eddie would help me. Maybe we could scare Mrs. Cooper somehow. Give her a dose of her own medicine!

When they finished the dishes, Mama carried the clean milk bottles out to the porch to leave for the milkman. When she came back, she said, "You'd better check on your snake before you get ready for bed. Make sure that screen's on tight!"

Janet went out to check the snake, and suddenly she knew how she would take her revenge. And soon.

Chapter 11

1934

Revenge

"Where's Mama?" asked Donnie, flinging his book bag on the couch.

Janet sat on the living room floor with Patty on her lap, pushing her squirmy sister's foot into one of her tiny sandals. Patty was struggling to free herself from Janet's arms. "Mama's in her bedroom, sewing," said Janet, holding tightly to Patty as she reached for another sandal.

Donnie went to find his mother, and then he came back to Janet. "Mama's got stuff all over the room," he said. "I bet she's gonna make a hundred costumes!"

Janet smiled. "It does looks that way, but she's just busy." She stood Patty on her feet and took her by the hand. "Donnie," she called over her shoulder, "don't go off anywhere. As long as Patty's had her nap, we're going to take her out in the wagon."

"Where?"

"Up the alley. Eddie's over at Nicky's, and I need to see both of them."

In a few minutes they were heading up the alley with Patty in the Radio Flyer. Donnie insisted on pulling, so Janet walked alongside him. She found Eddie and Nicky on Nicky's back porch. Butch was there, too.

Mary Ann, Nicky's little sister, came running over. She was about Donnie's age, with curls all over her head like Shirley Temple. Janet thought she was cute, but Nicky said she was a pest.

"Can I ride?" asked Mary Ann.

"Sure," said Donnie. "Move up, Patty."

Patty slid forward in the wagon, and Mary Ann scrambled in behind her, circling her arms around Patty's waist. "Giddee-yup, horse!" said Mary Ann.

"Gee-yup, hoss!" echoed Patty.

Donnie looked up at Janet. "Can I take them down to the end of the alley?" he asked. "I'll be careful."

Good, thought Janet. *Then we can talk in private.* "Okay," she replied, "and take your time."

Donnie turned the wagon around and started off. By that time the boys had left the porch and joined Janet. She was going to have to talk fast before the little kids came back.

"What's up?" asked Eddie, perching on a sawhorse in the driveway.

"Got an idea," said Janet, joining him. She grinned mischievously. "A way to get back at Mrs. Cooper."

"Yeah?" he asked. Nicky and Butch came closer.

"We could scare her," said Janet.

"Scare her?" asked Nicky.

"Yep. Make her hair stand on end, the old meanie."

Butch's eyes lit up. "By doing what?"

Janet lowered her voice and looked around. "I'll need everybody's help," she said. "And I can't let Donnie and Patty know, or they'll tell my mother."

"Yeah?" asked Butch.

"I'll need one of you to hold the ladder and the others to watch the kids."

"The ladder?" asked Butch. "What for?"

Janet grinned mischievously again. "You know that snake we caught?"

They nodded.

"My mother said I could keep it for a few days and then let it go, right? Well, I am going to let it go—straight into Mrs. Cooper's apartment!"

"What?" said Eddie, surprised.

"Stick it in through her kitchen window!" Janet clapped her hands over her mouth with glee.

Nicky leaned forward. "Isn't there a screen on her window?" he asked.

"Yeah, but it's one of those half-screens. She takes it out sometimes to shake her dustmop."

Eddie scratched his head. "I don't know, Jan," he said. "Letting the snake loose like that—well, I don't know . . ." Nicky and Butch were grinning, but Eddie wasn't. "I don't think you should," Eddie told her.

"Why not?"

"If you got caught, you'd probably get evicted!"

"I won't get caught," said Janet. "I'll do it while she's out."

"When?"

Janet shrugged her shoulders. "Soon. She always goes downtown on Friday afternoons. Maybe then." But she knew Mama would have to be away at the same time.

Eddie shook his head. "I don't know. Sounds crazy to me."

"It is crazy," said Nicky. "Crazy fun, that's what." He

stood up. "I'll help you," he said. "I've been wanting to get back at Old Lady Cooper ever since she evicted the Turners."

"Me, too!" said Butch, crossing his arms.

The Radio Flyer had returned, with Mary Ann pulling. Donnie hopped out, and Patty started to follow him.

"Gotta go," said Janet, running to catch Patty. "I'll let you know when!" she added.

"When what?" asked Donnie.

"When Santa Claus is coming," said Janet. "Hop in, Donnie! You get a free ride to the house."

As it turned out, the scheme was easier to pull off than Janet had expected. Mama told them at supper that she had to go over to Alice Peterson's on Saturday to deliver the first of the costumes.

Janet's eyes widened. *Saturday!* she thought. "I'll be glad to watch the kids," she said to Mama.

Her mother smiled. "Bless your heart. Janet, I don't know what I'd do without you."

Oh, Mama, thought Janet. *If you only knew.*

Twice each day during that week, Janet and Donnie caught insects for the snake and made sure the jar lid was full of clean water.

"You certainly are taking good care of that snake, Janet," said Mama. "But don't get too attached to it. Remember, you've got to let it go soon."

"I know, Mama," said Janet, smiling to herself. Then she thought, *Stay healthy, little snake. You have an important job to do!*

Mama already had her hat on when a letter arrived Saturday after lunch. She tore it open and read it quickly. "You'll be glad to hear your father's news," she said.

Janet ran over and picked up the envelope. She recognized Papa's careful printing on the outside.

"He did find another temporary job," said Mama. "But it's only for two weeks, so he'll be home soon!"

"Yippee!" yelled Janet and Donnie, hugging each other.

Their mother picked up her purse and headed for the living room. "I can't wait to tell him how well things are going here. He'll be so proud of us!" She opened the door to the hall. Patty followed and grabbed at her skirt. "No, honey," said Mama. "Take her, will you, Janet? I have to hurry, or I'll miss the streetcar." She hurried out, with the costumes over her arm.

Back inside, Janet pulled the letter out of the envelope. She read out loud to Donnie, "Dear Anna and Alla Barn." They giggled. "Alla barn" means "all the children" in Swedish. Papa knew Janet and Donnie would laugh when he called them that. He told them about the temporary job and that soon he would be back home with them. Donnie and Janet looked at each other and smiled. Then she read the rest:

> I'm sure you children are being good helpers and are keeping out of mischief.

Janet bit her lip.
"What else does it say?" demanded Donnie.

> Don't forget to obey Mrs. Cooper's rules. I want to have a home to come back to!
> With all my love,
> Papa

"We're being good, aren't we, Janet," said Donnie.

"Sure," she replied, stuffing the letter back into the envelope. She tossed it on the desk in the living room and tried not to think about it.

Someone knocked on the kitchen door, and Donnie ran to open it.

"Hi, squirt!" It was Nicky and Butch. "Let us in, quick! Your landlady doesn't want us around."

"It's okay," said Janet, coming into the kitchen. "Mrs. Cooper's not at home."

"Oh, yeah? Great!" They grinned at Janet.

"You seen Eddie?" asked Janet.

Nicky shook his head. "He's not home."

Nuts! thought Janet. Then she grinned. "My mother's not here either."

"What d'ya know!" said Nicky, winking.

"How's your snake doing?" asked Butch.

"Fine, just fine. Gonna have to let it go pretty soon, though."

"Really? Well, that's how it goes when you keep a snake," said Nicky. He was holding a bulging cloth bag by its drawstrings, and he set it on the floor near the kitchen door.

"What's that?" asked Janet.

"Mary Ann's blocks. She was taking them over to Punky Slominski's, but the kids all went off with their mother instead."

"Could Donnie and Patty play with the blocks for a little while?" Janet gave Nicky a determined look.

"Here?"

"Yeah." *Come on, Nicky,* thought Janet. *You know what we need to do!*

Nicky finally caught on. "Oh, yeah, sure!" He looked over at Butch. "You stay with the kids for a while, okay?"

"Why?"

"I have to help Janet with something." He gestured toward the backyard.

Butch nodded and led Patty and Donnie into the living room. Janet could hear their squeals as the blocks spilled out on the floor. She and Nicky scooted out the back door and around to the shed.

From the back of the shed, Mrs. Cooper's kitchen window was in plain view. The bottom half was propped open with a small wooden-framed screen.

"I see what you mean about that screen," said Nicky. "Should be easy to get it out."

But the sloping roof directly beneath the window made Janet wonder about taking the slippery glass fishbowl up there.

"Let's get the ladder first and then go back for the snake," she said.

They lugged the heavy ladder out of the shed and set it up along the side of the house, so no one would see them. Janet ran into the shed for the snake. When she came out, Nicky said, "I think I better go up first, so I can get that screen out."

Janet steadied the ladder with one hand and hugged the fishbowl with the other while Nicky climbed up. She looked down at the snake, coiled up and eyeing her steadily. She decided it might be safer to carry the snake up without the bowl. She set the bowl down on the grass.

Nicky carefully removed the screen. The window started to drop, but he held it open. The white ruffled curtains fluttered in the breeze. "Hurry up," he said. "I can't hold this thing forever."

Janet looked down at the snake, held her breath, and grabbed it right below the head. It felt colder than she expected, and she almost dropped it. Quickly, she mounted the rungs, holding the snake out in front of her. She tiptoed across the shingles and up to where Nicky was waiting.

"Okay, stick it in!" said Nicky.

Janet thrust her hand inside the curtains and let go of the snake. Nicky slapped the screen back into place and let the window drop down onto it.

They looked at each other. "Done!" said Janet. "Let's get out of here."

They put the ladder back in the shed and were hurrying across the backyard when the kitchen screen door flew open. "Janet!" yelled Donnie. "That lady's here! Mrs. Cooper's daughter!"

Chapter 12

1934

Stalling for Time

Janet ran over to the back porch where Donnie stood holding the door open.

"Where is she?" asked Janet, dashing past him.

"Out front," he called after her.

In the living room, Butch was adding a block to a high, wobbly tower. "Knock it down!" said Patty, clapping her hands.

"Keep it up, Butch," said Janet. She turned to Nicky. "You'd better stay inside," she said. "This lady might tell her mother you were here." She didn't wait for his answer.

Sylvia stood near the front porch railing, studying the street below. She turned and smiled when Janet came through the screen door. Her blue dress matched her eyes.

Janet grinned. "Nice to see you," she said, hoping Sylvia wouldn't notice how out of breath she was. Why did she have to come around just now? she wondered.

"Sorry to bother you, but my mother's out, and I don't have a key."

Janet nodded. "Gone shopping, I think."

"I should have remembered," said Sylvia. "She goes every Saturday, doesn't she?"

Janet nodded again. "I think so."

"Any idea when she'll be back?"

"I don't really know." Janet hesitated, and then she said, "You wanna come in?" Mama always invited people in, but what if she said yes? She could feel her heart pounding as she thought about the snake.

"I'll wait outside, thanks," said Sylvia, looking around. "Over there, I guess."

Janet watched with envy as Sylvia crossed the porch and arranged herself in a green wooden swing that the Larson children were not allowed to touch.

Sylvia smoothed her skirt. "Sure brings back memories," she said, leaning back and looking around. "I grew up here, you know." A ruffle around the hem of her skirt fluttered slightly as the swing creaked.

"You lived here?" asked Janet, moving closer. "On the first floor or the second?"

Sylvia smiled. "Oh, in the whole house."

Like back in Columbia Heights, thought Janet. Her mind was racing. She had to keep Sylvia on the porch until she could figure out what to do next.

"Well, Janet," said Sylvia, "you want to sit down?" Sylvia moved over slightly on the swing.

Janet withdrew ever so slightly. "We're not allowed."

The woman's thin eyebrows arched. "Really?" She frowned, and then she said, "Well, I'm sure it's all right as long as I'm here." After Janet was settled in the swing, Sylvia asked, "Do you go to Howard School?"

"Yep."

"So did I!" said Sylvia. "Is Miss Jamison still there?

She was my favorite."

"That's my teacher!" said Janet, delighted.

"Fifth grade, right?"

"Yep." She kept checking for Mrs. Cooper out of the corner of her eye.

"Seems like yesterday," said Sylvia, pulling a silver cigarette case and lighter from her purse. Janet watched, fascinated, as Sylvia flipped the case open. A row of cigarettes lay strapped inside like little white mummies. She slipped one out, tapped an end against the case, and pressed the cigarette between her lips. She flicked a switch on the lighter, and a small flame licked at the cigarette until it glowed bright red. Sylvia blew out a puff of smoke and dropped the case and lighter back into her purse. A glass-beaded bracelet jingled at her wrist.

"Yes sir," said Sylvia, leaning back again, "this place holds a lot of memories for me—and for Mother, too. That's why it was so hard on her."

"Hard on her?" asked Janet.

"She's never gotten over it, really." Sylvia took another puff and sat fiddling with her bracelet.

"Gotten over what?" asked Janet, knitting her eyebrows together.

"The stock market crash and losing my father. One right after the other, just like that. Most of their money went down the drain." Sylvia sighed. "I wanted her to come live with me, but she insisted on staying here in her own place. Couldn't sell the house though—nobody's buying houses these days—so she rents the downstairs to make ends meet . . ." Sylvia stared off into the distance as she talked. "First family that came made a real mess of this place, and the second . . . well, those kids were hellions, tore up the lawn and yelled all the time. Poor Mother was almost beside herself."

Janet sat cracking her knuckles slowly.

Sylvia glanced over at her. "Oh, but don't worry. She was very happy when your family came. She knew right away you'd be just perfect for that apartment."

Janet swallowed hard.

"There may be problems with the kids in the neighborhood, though," Sylvia continued. "Mother says the new ones seem to be, well, kind of a rough bunch."

"Really?" Janet sat up straight in the swing.

Sylvia went on to tell her that her mother had had a heart condition for years. "She doesn't like to admit it, though," said Sylvia. "Guess she's afraid I'll make her come and live with me." She took a long puff on the cigarette and continued. "When she got so upset over that last family, I was worried sick she'd have another heart attack."

Janet's eyes widened. "A heart attack?"

"Yes. Doctor said she must never get overexcited or unduly upset. Next one could be fatal."

Fatal! thought Janet. Oh, my goodness! She felt her stomach tighten into a ball. "Excuse me," she said, jumping down from the swing. "I have to go inside."

"Are you all right?" asked Sylvia.

"Yes, but I have to check on my little brother and sister."

Sylvia looked at her watch. "Tell you what," she said, getting up. "I need a few things from the store. I'll run down there right now, and maybe Mother will be here when I get back."

"Hope so," said Janet. *No I don't,* she thought. *I hope it takes her forever.*

"Oh," said Sylvia, reaching into her purse as she stood by the steps. "These are for the little kids." She brought out two boxes of animal crackers with string handles. "And a pack of gum for you," she said.

Chapter Twelve

"Oh, thank you!" said Janet, turning over the shiny pack in her hand. She had never had a whole pack to herself. And the animal crackers couldn't have come at a better time! They might just save the day.

Janet dashed inside, where everyone was still busy with the blocks. She gave out the animal crackers and motioned for Nicky to follow her out the back door. "Hurry! We've got to get the snake back!" she called over her shoulder.

"What? Why?"

Janet told him about Mrs. Cooper's heart when they got into the shed.

"We might not find that snake," said Nicky, shaking his head. "It's mighty small."

"We've got to!" They lugged the ladder over to the shed. In a few moments Janet was holding up the window. Nicky lifted out the screen. "What if Old Lady Cooper comes home while we're in there?" he asked.

"You watch for her, and I'll do the looking!" said Janet. She ducked her head through the starched curtains and stepped inside. She was in Mrs. Cooper's kitchen.

Chapter 13

1934

Capture

To Janet's surprise, the landlady's kitchen was only half the size of her family's downstairs. She and Nicky dropped to their knees to search for Samantha. They checked under the enamel sink, the kerosene stove, and behind a broom that stood in a corner. No snake.

"I'll look under the icebox," said Janet. "You'd better go in the living room and listen for Mrs. Cooper." Nicky disappeared through the open doorway.

Janet slid the heavy drip pan out from under the icebox and peered into the darkness underneath. She couldn't see anything, so she pulled the shade from a small table lamp and laid the lamp on the floor.

"Come on, Samantha, where are you?" she called, but there was no snake—just cobwebs and a dusty pencil. Janet pushed the pan back under the icebox and returned the lamp to the table.

Nicky stuck his head in the doorway. "Nobody around," he said.

"Keep watching," said Janet as she headed for the bedroom. She looked under all the furniture. No snake anywhere in sight. Then she went into the bathroom. It looked exactly like theirs downstairs: rust-stained sink, pull chain toilet, and the same claw-footed bathtub. Janet knelt down and peered under the tub. And there in a dark corner lay the snake, coiled up and watching her.

"I FOUND IT!" she yelled to Nicky. Each of them tried to reach it, but it was too far back under the tub. Janet got the broom and slid the handle toward Samantha. The snake slithered sideways. Each time she moved the broom handle, the snake moved until finally it stretched itself out under the center of the tub. Janet took a deep breath and grabbed its clammy body. Holding the startled snake out in front of her, she and Nicky bolted back into the kitchen. Janet peeked out through the flapping window curtains. No one seemed to be around down below.

"Hurry up," said Nicky. "I'll put the screen back when we get out."

Janet stepped over the windowsill and out onto the slanting shed roof. For a few dizzying seconds she glanced down into the backyard, half-fearing Mrs. Cooper might come storming up the alley.

"What're you doing?" asked a high voice. It was Nicky's little sister. She stood with one hand on her hip, shading her eyes from the late afternoon sun.

"Nothing," said Janet, hustling down the ladder. Nicky was right behind her.

"What have you got?" asked Mary Ann.

"None of your business," snapped Nicky. "Beat it, kid!"

"I'm telling!" said Mary Ann, turning to leave.

Nicky ran over and stuck his fist under her chin.

"You do and I'll tell Ma how you snitched candy from the store!"

Mary Ann's face crumpled, and she turned and ran.

Janet circled a bush and tossed the snake behind it. Then she helped Nicky ease the wooden ladder away from the roof and down to the ground. He and Janet each grabbed one end and lugged it back into the shed. "You better scram," said Janet, slamming the creaking door. "Thanks for helping."

Nicky grinned. "Any time!" He took off down the alley.

Janet sprinted over to the back door and flung it open. Patty came toddling into the kitchen. "Mama?" she asked.

"No, it's me," said Janet, whisking Patty back into the living room. Butch and Donnie were dumping the last of the blocks into the bag.

Donnie looked up at Janet. "We made a fort," he said.

"Patchey fort," said Patty, clapping her hands.

"Fort Apache," said Donnie, smugly.

Butch pulled the drawstrings and closed the bag. "Everything okay?" he asked Janet.

"Mission accomplished," she said, winking. "Thanks for watching them, Butch."

Butch had just slipped out the back door when Mrs. Cooper came up the walk. Janet was in the front hall telling her about Sylvia's visit when Mama returned, too. She came inside, breathless. "Alice loved the costumes!" she said. "One of the skirts has to be shortened a little, but other than that, they fit perfectly!"

Mrs. Cooper smiled. "When is that Swedish festival again?"

"The twentieth of June," said Mama," but the costumes have to be ready a week ahead of time. I've really got to keep at it from now on."

"It's a good thing you have Janet to watch those little ones," Mrs. Cooper said, eyeing Janet.

Yeah, thought Janet, *she thinks it keeps me out of mischief.*

While they were eating supper, Janet told Mama about Sylvia's visit. "She told me Mrs. Cooper has a bad heart," said Janet.

"I'm not surprised," said Mama. "She's pretty elderly, you know."

Donnie looked puzzled. "How can a heart be naughty?" he asked.

Janet rolled her eyes. "Not naughty, dummy. Bad, like an old battery."

"Good comparison," said Mama.

"Well, anyway," continued Janet, "Sylvia said her mother had a heart attack once, and she could die if she had another one."

"Yippee!" said Donnie, clapping. "The end of Mrs. Cooper!"

"Shhh! For heaven's sake, Donnie, keep your voice down!" said Mama. "That's not funny. We may not like Mrs. Cooper, but we certainly wouldn't want her to die."

"I would," Donnie shot back. "So would Janet!"

"I would not!"

"You would, too! You hate her. I heard you."

"Children! That's enough!" said Mama. "Of course Janet wouldn't want Mrs. Cooper to die. Now let's not hear any more about it."

Janet stuck her tongue out at Donnie, but he just sat mashing his peas.

Suddenly Mama said, "Janet, have you fed that snake today?"

Janet set her milk glass down slowly and tried to sound casual. "I let it go this afternoon."

Donnie dropped his fork. "You didn't tell me you were gonna."

"You were playing," said Janet, flipping her hair back. "Besides, you know Mama said we couldn't keep it."

Donnie sat pouting, and a big tear rolled down his cheek. Mama said, "You could at least have told your brother first. He helped you a lot with that snake."

Janet shoved her chair back. "I can't win around here!" she said. "You told me I couldn't keep it, and when I let it go, I get yelled at!" She fled to the bathroom, slammed the door with all her might, and locked it.

In a few moments someone knocked rapidly, and she heard Mama's voice. "Open the door, Janet."

"No!"

"I want to talk to you."

"Well, I don't want to talk to you!"

"Janet, come out here right now."

Janet finally opened the door, which led into the room she shared with Patty. Mama sat down wearily on the bed. "I know you were angry, Jan, but I can't have you slamming the bathroom door like that."

"I don't have a bedroom door to slam!" snapped Janet, glancing at the faded curtain that separated her room from the rest of the apartment.

"You know what I mean. And at least you still have a bedroom." Mama stood up and turned to Janet. "Remember," she said, "if it happened to the Turners, it could happen to us." Her voice broke, and Janet saw tears in her mother's eyes as she left the room.

The next afternoon, Janet was in her backyard when she caught a glimpse of Eddie through the picket fence. He was on his knees weeding a flower garden and didn't notice her until she called to him. "Where've you been, Eddie?" she asked.

Eddie looked up and smiled. "Around. Why?" He squinted at her in the bright sunlight.

"You missed some excitement here yesterday," said Janet, grinning back mischievously. She leaned over the fence and told him all about putting the snake in Mrs. Cooper's kitchen, about the landlady's heart condition, and how she and Nicky had gone back and found the snake. She described everything, down to the last detail. "Too bad you weren't here," she said to Eddie.

Eddie picked up a trowel and started digging up a dandelion. "It's probably better I wasn't home," he said.

"Why?"

He shrugged. "I told you I didn't think scaring Mrs. Cooper was a good idea."

Janet glanced at the landlady's window, and then she remembered that Mrs. Cooper had gone downtown. "Eddie, you know what she's like. She's . . . she's just like a gangster!"

Eddie sat back on his heels and tapped the grass slowly with his trowel. He kept his eyes down for a few moments, and finally he looked up. "Jan," he said, "does your priest ever talk about loving your enemies?"

Janet smiled. "We don't have priests. We have ministers."

"Your minister then."

She shrugged. "Sure. So what?"

"Well, Father Cronin says we should try to think of why enemies are mean. Maybe something happened to them that makes them want to hurt other people. Or maybe they just don't know any better."

"Well, Mrs. Cooper knows better. And if she doesn't, she should!"

"And scaring her would have made her change?"

Janet crossed her arms. "I didn't expect her to change. I just wanted to get back at her for being such a meanie!" She looked up at Mrs. Cooper's window, half expecting her to be watching. Then she looked back across the fence. "Besides," she added, "this is only temporary."

"What do you mean?"

"My father said we're not going to live here that long." She flipped her hair back and said, "We're gonna move as soon as he gets a job."

Eddie stood up. "But meanwhile, if your landlady ever found out about that snake, your whole family would be out on the street!"

"Look, Eddie," said Janet, clenching her fists, "I don't need any lectures from you. You don't know what it's like living in the same house with that old lady!"

Eddie glared at her. "Well, if you want to be stupid about it, go ahead. Just remember, I warned you."

Janet could feel her eyes filling up. "You don't care how I feel, do you?"

"I didn't say that. I just think it was a dumb thing to do."

"Well, I don't! It's time someone got back at her!"

Eddie just shook his head and went back to his weeding. Janet waited a few moments with her hands on her hips. Then she tossed her head and marched back into the house.

Chapter 14

1934

Emergency

For three weeks, Mama had worked on the costumes every afternoon while Patty was napping and whenever Janet was at home and could watch both Patty and Donnie. Janet had gotten used to the clickety-clack of the sewing machine at night, too, as she drifted off to sleep. She wondered if her mother ever went to bed.

"Well," Mama announced finally, "next Tuesday I'll be taking the last of the costumes over to the dance studio."

"On the streetcar?" asked Janet, trying to imagine her struggling up the metal steps with costumes piled up to her nose.

Mama smiled. "Alice is going to pick me up."

"Oh, boy! Can we go, too?" asked Donnie. A ride in a car was a rare treat.

"PLEASE, Mama!" begged Janet. "We want to see the dancers wear the costumes!"

Mama shook her head. "I know you'd love to go, but

I don't think Alice wants children hanging around the studio. Can you imagine Patty in a place like that?"

Janet slumped down on the couch. She thought, *And I get to watch the kids again. I'm so sick of this!*

Donnie stood twisting a lock of his hair. "We can go to the real festival, though, can't we, Mama?" he asked.

"I'm afraid not," said Mama wistfully. "Tickets cost fifty cents apiece." She looked over at Janet. "Would you believe that?"

Janet shook her head. "Fifty cents!" she said. "Our whole family could go to the movies for that!"

On Tuesday, as Mama was putting the costumes on their hangers, Mrs. Cooper came down and asked to borrow the Larsons' step stool. "Lent mine to the Turners," she sniffed. "The people from the sheriff's office must have dumped it on the sidewalk along with all the rest of their stuff. I know I never saw it after they left."

Mama got the step stool. "Anything I can help you with?" she asked, looking nervously at the clock.

"No, thank you," said the landlady. "Just want to do the kitchen windows while the weather's good."

Mama insisted on carrying the stool upstairs, and when she returned, she said, "I hope that woman knows what she's doing, climbing up to do those windows like that." She shook her head. "Stubborn, just like your grandmother used to be. Never would admit she needed any help."

Later, Janet and Donnie sat eating the lunch Mama had fixed for them before Alice honked the horn of her car from the street. The house was quiet with Mama gone and Patty napping. Their little sister was sleeping on Mama and Papa's bed on the sun porch, so at least there was a door to close. It didn't take much to wake up Patty these days, now that she knew school was out.

"What are you gonna do after lunch?" Donnie asked, digging the raisin face out of his applesauce.

Janet pushed back her bowl. "Not much, as long as I have to watch you and Patty." She sighed. "Won't seem like summer vacation until Mama's finished with all this."

"Well, the festival's this Sunday."

"Yeah, I know." Janet sat fiddling with her spoon. "But just you wait and see. Mama will probably come back today with some more work to—"

There was a loud thud overhead. Donnie looked up. "Mrs. Cooper musta dropped something heavy," he said.

"Yeah," said Janet. She grinned. "I think I'll go tell her she's making too much noise."

Then Donnie froze. "What's that?"

"What?"

"Shhh! Listen!" He leaned forward. "She's moaning!"

Janet rolled her eyes. "Oh, come on, Donnie, don't be silly."

"She is! Listen!"

Janet cocked her head. Donnie was right. Now she could hear it, too—faint moans from upstairs. It could hardly be anyone but Mrs. Cooper.

"What should we do?" asked Donnie, sitting up straight.

Janet shrugged. "I dunno. I guess maybe we could go up and check."

Donnie shoved his chair back. "We better!" he said.

Janet followed Donnie through the front hall and up the stairs. They tried the door. Locked. They knocked and waited. No answer. They banged hard a few times. Nothing.

Donnie looked at Janet, wide-eyed. "Maybe she's dead!"

Janet shook her head. "Don't be ridiculous. She probably just can't get up!"

When they got back down to the kitchen, they could still hear Mrs. Cooper. Janet said she'd try getting in through her kitchen window.

"You can't do that!" said Donnie.

"You wanna bet? I can with a ladder!"

Donnie followed her outside, but Janet turned to him. "You better stay in the house. Patty might wake up."

"She just went to sleep," Donnie whined. "I want to go, too!"

"No!" she called over her shoulder. "Get back inside!"

"You can't make me!"

Janet whirled around and glared at her little brother. "Get back in there, and you can have my last stick of gum. It's in my top dresser drawer."

"Oh, boy!" Donnie darted back toward the house.

Janet ran around to the back of the shed and yanked on the door. It creaked open, and a daddy longlegs sprinted out. The wooden ladder still lay along the wall where she and Nicky had dumped it. She managed to drag it outside, but by then her arms were beginning to ache. Raising it up against the roof would be impossible.

Janet looked over at the Polzacs'. She hadn't seen Eddie since their exchange over the fence, so she ran up to Nicky's instead.

Nicky and Butch were throwing darts against a homemade target. "What's wrong?" asked Nicky, as soon as he saw Janet's face.

"I need your help! It's Mrs. Cooper!" She motioned for them to follow as she headed back down the alley.

"What's that old bat up to now?" asked Nicky,

falling into step beside Janet.

"Nothing—I mean, I think she's hurt—and maybe bad!"

"Where is she?" asked Butch, puffing along behind them.

"Upstairs. Her door's locked. I need help with the ladder."

Moments later she and Nicky had the ladder in place against the house. "Pays to have practice," said Nicky, checking to be sure it was steady.

Janet turned to Butch. "Do you think you . . ."

"I know, watch the kids, right?"

"Please, Butch? Donnie's in there by himself, and Patty might wake up." She started up the ladder, relieved to see Butch going inside the house.

Nicky followed Janet, and in a few moments they were in Mrs. Cooper's kitchen. The landlady lay on the floor next to the step stool, and she was very quiet.

Janet knelt down next to her. She looked small and fragile, lying so still on the floor. Janet hesitated a moment, and then she reached out and put her hand on the woman's shoulder. "Mrs. Cooper," she said, "it's me, Janet."

Mrs. Cooper's eyes fluttered open and then closed again. There was a bloody gash on her temple and blood on her housedress. Janet shuddered. "See if you can find a blanket, Nicky," she said. She remembered from a movie that people should be kept warm when they're injured. Janet stayed close by.

Nicky came back with an afghan from the couch. They tucked it around Mrs. Cooper, who stirred slightly as they did.

"What shall we do?" Janet asked Nicky. "She needs help."

Nicky shrugged. "There's a telephone in the living room," he said. "Know how to use one?"

Janet headed out of the kitchen. "We had one a long time ago," she said. "You just listen for the operator and tell her what number you want."

"Who should we call?" asked Nicky, following her.

"The hospital, I guess."

Janet picked up the telephone gingerly and lifted the receiver from its hook. When she put it to her ear, though, someone said, "And then Edith came over and the . . ."

Janet leaned down and spoke loudly into the mouthpiece. "Hello?" she said.

"I'm on the line," came a voice.

"I'd like the operator, please."

"I said I'm on the line. Would you please get off?"

"Hello?" said Janet again. "I need the operator."

"Look, kid, get off the phone."

Janet clapped her hand over the mouthpiece. "What'll I do?" she asked. "Someone's on the line."

Nicky rolled his eyes. "Tell them it's an emergency."

"It's an emergency!" shouted Janet.

"Sure, kid, that's what everyone says. You get off this line before I report you!"

Janet slammed the receiver back on the hook and looked at Nicky. "Now what'll we do?"

Chapter 15

1934

Alone with Mrs. Cooper

Mrs. Cooper moaned again from the kitchen. Suddenly Janet remembered Eddie's telephone. "Mrs. Polzac said we could use their phone in an emergency," she said.

"I'll go over!" said Nicky. He dashed out the door.

Janet ran back to the kitchen. The landlady still lay with her eyes closed, her face as white as the cleaning rag she was still clutching. Janet knelt down beside her again. Was she still breathing? Janet couldn't tell, and that made her own breath almost stop. What if Mrs. Cooper died right there in front of her?

Janet pressed her hand against the landlady's chest. She couldn't feel a heartbeat. Oh, no, God! she prayed. Please don't let her die! She pressed again, and this time she felt a faint thump-thump-thump. It was slow and weak, but it was there. She sighed with relief.

Janet looked at the gash on Mrs. Cooper's head. She thought it might still be bleeding, so she looked for a clean washcloth and found one on a shelf in the bathroom. She ran back to the landlady, planning to hold the cloth firmly against the cut, as Mama always did, to stop the bleeding. Something inside her, though, pulled her back from the blood, and she had to force herself to touch the wound. When she did, Mrs. Cooper opened her eyes and moaned a little, and then closed them again. Janet bit her lip and somehow managed to keep the washcloth in place.

As Janet knelt there on the floor, her eyes fell on a framed photograph that stood on a small chest near the doorway. The picture looked as if it had been taken in the front yard of their house, but the tree next to the porch was just a small one. A tall man stood with a pipe in his hand, and a little girl in a long white dress sat on the lap of a smiling young woman in a high-collared blouse and a long dark skirt.

Janet looked harder at the picture. To her amazement, the woman looked like Mrs. Cooper! Her hair was dark and wavy, not gray and pinned back as she wore it now, but her eyes were the same, small and dark, and she had the same heavy eyebrows. She looked happy, and pretty.

Janet looked down at the wrinkled woman who lay whimpering alongside her. Could Mrs. Cooper, whom Janet always thought of as a mean old lady, once have been that smiling young woman? When did she change? When her husband died? When they lost their money? Or was it when other people started living in her house—like those kids who tore up her lawn? Janet decided it must have been everything all rolled up in one. Well, she sure was a grouch by the time the Larsons moved in!

Janet looked around at the tiny kitchen with its sloping ceiling and one little window. *I guess it would be pretty lonely*, she thought, *to hear people laughing and having fun downstairs when you're stuck up here all by yourself—and the whole house used to be yours.* And to know that one of those people . . . Janet sat biting her nail.

Suddenly, all the hurtful things between the two of them seemed to melt away. To her surprise, Mrs. Cooper didn't look like just an old lady anymore. Janet could see a young, smiling woman in her face, too. *Maybe that's it,* she thought. *Maybe that's what God sees—what we used to be, what we are now, and what we can be.* Janet swallowed hard. She looked up at the sunlight streaming through the kitchen window. *I can't help what's already happened to Mrs. Cooper,* she thought, *but from now on I'm going to see that nothing I do makes her—or anyone else—worse off than they were before.*

The downstairs door opened, and people came stomping up the stairs. Nicky, Eddie, and Mrs. Polzac rushed in and soon surrounded Janet and Mrs. Cooper.

"The hospital's sending an ambulance," said Eddie, patting Janet on the shoulder.

"Good," said Janet, smiling gratefully at him.

Eddie's mother leaned down close to the landlady. "Mrs. Cooper?" she said loudly.

This time the woman's eyes stayed open briefly. "Mrs. Cooper," said Mrs. Polzac again, lowering her voice, "just try to relax if you can. We've sent for help."

"Thank you," mumbled the landlady. They could barely hear her, but Janet saw that she smiled weakly. Just like in the picture.

New Beginnings

When Mama returned home late that afternoon, the first thing she heard was that Mrs. Cooper was in the hospital. The kitchen was full of neighborhood children, all of them chattering at once about the arrival of the ambulance and how some men had taken Mrs. Cooper down the front steps on a stretcher.

"There were wheels on it," said Donnie.

"Yeah, and they had her strapped down," added Butch, nodding.

"Why did they do that?" asked Donnie. "So she couldn't get away?"

Janet rolled her eyes. "No, dummy, so she wouldn't fall off."

Eddie added, "She wasn't even awake by that time."

Mama frowned. "Has anybody heard whether she's going to be all right?"

Janet shook her head. "We don't know yet. We're waiting to hear from Sylvia. Eddie's mother found her number in the telephone book and called her."

Donnie said, "And Mrs. Polzac stayed at the hospital till she got there."

"That was certainly nice of her," said Mama, tying on her apron.

Someone knocked at the door. It was Mrs. Polzac, bearing a large kettle. "Thought you might need a little help with dinner," she said, smiling at Mama. "Janet's been telling me how you've worked every spare minute on all those costumes." She presented the kettle to Mama and stepped back.

Mama thanked her, bewildered, and set the kettle on the stove. She lifted the lid and sniffed. "Mmm! This smells wonderful!" she said. "How kind of you!"

Mrs. Polzac smiled again. "A chicken goes a long way when you throw some vegetables in with it." She looked around awkwardly. This was the first time she had ever been in the Larsons' apartment.

"I bet there's dill in this," said Mama, sniffing again over the steaming kettle. "I never thought of using dill with chicken."

Mrs. Polzac smoothed her apron. "It's called *kur-czeta*," she said proudly. "My mother's specialty back in Poland."

Janet watched the two women with interest. She hadn't seen her mother chat with a neighbor since they left Columbia Heights.

Mama put the lid back on the kettle. "I hope you'll give me the recipe," she said.

"Be glad to," said Eddie's mother.

Janet beamed at Mama. "It's almost like Columbia Heights," she said.

"What?"

Chapter Sixteen

Janet shrugged and grinned. "I mean, remember how you used to trade recipes with Mrs. Munson?"

Her mother nodded. "I hadn't realized how much I missed it."

They joined the others around the kitchen table, and everyone started telling Mama how Janet and Nicky had rescued Mrs. Cooper by climbing into her window. Mrs. Polzac said, "Would you believe those children had the presence of mind to get a ladder and climb up there like that?"

"Incredible!" said Mama, proudly.

Janet and Nicky glanced at each other and Nicky said, "I guess when it's an emergency, you just do it, that's all." Eddie grinned at them both and winked.

Janet moved over next to her mother. "I hope Mrs. Cooper's going to be okay," she said. And she meant it. She looked down a moment and blinked back her tears. "It's gonna be different around here from now on," she said, looking back up at Mama. "I promise."

Her mother smiled and nodded, dabbing at her eyes. "And I promise, too," she said, but she was looking at Mrs. Polzac. She smiled at her neighbor. "I hope you'll call me Anna from now on."

Mrs. Polzac beamed and replied, "And I'm Marie."

Just then someone knocked on the back door. It was Eddie's older brother George to say that Sylvia had called from the hospital. "She said to tell everyone that her mother has a mild concussion, but she can come home tomorrow." He looked around at all the smiling faces and added, "And . . . let's see . . . she said something else." George scratched his head. "Oh yeah, I remember. She wanted to invite all of you—everyone who helped her—to some kind of a festival next week."

Janet looked at Mama and held her breath.

George continued, "It's a Swedish midsummer festival, and everyone's going to be dressed up in costumes."

Donnie clapped his hands. "I knew we could go! I knew we could go!"

Mama's eyebrows shot up. "Mrs. Cooper's doing that for us?"

"Yeah. She said it's her way of saying thank you to everybody and 'welcome to the neighborhood,' or something like that."

"Well, I declare!" said Mama and Mrs. Polzac at the same time.

Donnie looked confused. "Butch and Nicky didn't just move here," he said.

"It's never too late to welcome anyone," said Mama quietly.

George turned to leave, but he paused when he opened the back door. "You expecting anyone?" he asked. "There's a truck pulling up."

A-oogah! A-oogah! went the horn.

Janet jumped up. "It's Papa!"

History in Real Life:
The Great Depression

In January 1934, when *A Better Tomorrow?* begins, the United States of America was in the midst of one of the saddest periods of its history. Only a few years earlier, during the Roaring Twenties, most people were working, and many were buying new homes and cars. Big business prospered, and wealthy businessmen made front page news, along with movie stars and athletes. Times were the best they had ever been, and most people thought they could only get better.

But many Americans began to take chances. They borrowed money and took risks in the stock market. Then stocks prices tumbled and the market "crashed" late in 1929. When that happened, factories, shops, and offices went out of business, and the millions of people who had worked in them lost their jobs. Without money to pay their mortgages, those same people also lost their homes.

The small salaries that most workers received in those days had not allowed them to set aside money for emergencies. And those who had been able to save soon found that they had lost their money when even the banks failed and had to close. There was no such thing then as Social Security or federal government programs to help people who were out of work. Individual states did what they could to help, but soon that money was used up. Most city governments could not even pay the salaries of teachers and policemen, let alone feed starving people. Breadlines and soup kitchens, sponsored by churches and private institutions, became an everyday sight.

In 1934, Congress finally provided money to create federal programs that brought jobs and relief to millions of Americans. As people began working again, factories were able to reopen, creating more jobs, and more people could buy the goods that were once again becoming available in the stores. Also, laws were passed that helped people buy homes and farms again. All of this took time, however, and years passed before the Depression that had caused so much suffering in America and around the world finally came to an end.

Those who lived through America's lean years never forgot how quickly times could change and that even the kindest and the best people can suddenly become poor through no fault of their own.

During the depths of the Depression, it was common for many Americans to become hopeless and despondent. Some even committed suicide rather than face reality. Others, however, refused to give in to despair. They managed to keep a long-range view of what had happened to them. They instilled in themselves—and consequently in their children—a conviction that there would indeed be a better tomorrow. They survived by trusting that their present situation, terrible though it might be, was only temporary. As indeed it was.

Read More about It

To find out more about the Great Depression, check your local library for these titles:

Fiction

Burch, Robert. *Ida Early Comes Over the Mountain.* New York: Viking Press, 1980.
Tough times in rural Georgia during the Depression take a lively turn when spirited Ida Early arrives to keep house for the Suttons.

Crofford, Emily. *A Matter of Pride.* Minneapolis: Carolrhoda Books, 1981.
A young girl's opinion of her mother changes as she watches the woman display her courage during the Depression.

Crofford, Emily. *A Place to Belong.* Minneapolis: Carolrhoda Books, 1994.
In 1935, sixth grader Talmadge struggles to endure his harsh new life on an Arkansas plantation.

Greene, Constance C. Dotty's Suitcase. New York: Viking Press, 1980.
During the Depression, twelve-year-old Dotty's dream of traveling seems remote until she finds money from a bank robbery.

Lyon, George Ella. *Borrowed Children.* New York: Orchard Books, 1988.
Twelve-year-old Amanda has a holiday in Memphis, far removed from the Depression drudgery of her Kentucky mountain family.

Thrasher, Crystal. *The Dark Didn't Catch Me.* New York: Atheneum, 1975.
Seeley withstands the work, troubles, and sorrows that encompass her family in southern Indiana during the Depression.

Turner, Ann Warren. *Dust for Dinner.* New York: HarperCollins, 1995.
Jake tells the story of his family's life in the Oklahoma dust bowl and the journey to California during the Great Depression.

Nonfiction

Glassman, Bruce. *The Crash of '29 and the New Deal.* Morristown, N.J.: Silver Burdett Co., 1986.
This book examines the time period of American history from the Roaring twenties through the financial rebuilding of the New Deal.

Katz, William Loren. *An Album of the Great Depression.* New York: F. Watts, 1978.
This book discusses the causes, events, and effects of the Great Depression and highlights programs designed to alleviate it.

Rublowsky, John. *After the Crash; America in the Great Depression.* New York: Crowell-Collier Press, 1970.
This book discusses the events and economic conditions that brought about the Depression.

About the Author

Dorothy Lilja Harrison has loved hearing and reading stories ever since she was a little girl. Later, when she grew up and had two boys and two girls of her own, she shared her love of books with her children, as well as with the kindergartners she taught. Now, she has taken that love to the next level—she has authored the books of the Chronicles of Courage series.

A Better Tomorrow? is not a true story, but it might have been, for millions of families were living through hard times in those days. The house and neighborhood where the "Larsons" lived, and the church that they attended, are just like those Dorothy remembers from her childhood in Minneapolis during the Great Depression.

Today, Mrs. Harrison lives in Ellicott City, Maryland, with her husband, a retired United Methodist pastor. Their grown children have become a musician, an artist, an editor, and a nurse. Their two grandchildren live nearby.

Operation Morningstar

"Children shouldn't be traveling without adults—it's too dangerous these days."

That's what the five Mueller children keep hearing as they make their way across war-torn Germany in search of their father and three younger sisters.

World War Two has just ended, and Katrina, Rudy, Heidi, Helga, and Volfie have just five days to reach their father and sisters before they leave for America. The Muellers have mapped out their journey, and if they stick to their schedule, they should make it. What they haven't planned for are road blocks, unfriendly American soldiers, and spending a night in jail. They have very little food and money, and only their feet to move them. Their hearts are set on finding their father and sisters, but will they reach them in time?

"Please, God!" Katrina prays, "Please help us!"

Based on a true story, *Operation Morningstar* is an exciting adventure you won't want to miss!

Be sure to read all three books in the
Chronicles of Courage series:
A Better Tomorrow?
Operation Morningstar
Gold in the Garden

ChariotVICTOR
◆ **PUBLISHING** ◆
A DIVISION OF COOK COMMUNICATIONS

Gold in the Garden

Death was not something I had thought about very much . . . at least not until Susan died.

Kathy Jordan has a secret, one she is sure she can never tell. Her best friend, Susan, has died, and she believes it's her fault. If she tells anyone, she's sure she'll never have a friend again. After all, how could anyone—even God— love a person who caused her best friend's death?

A tender story of healing and forgiveness, *Gold in the Garden* reaches back to the days of the early 1950s when polio swept the nation. Many parents feared for the lives of their children. As you read, you'll discover along with Kathy that healing is possible for even the worst wounds of the heart.

Be sure to read all three books in the
Chronicles of Courage series:
A Better Tomorrow?
Operation Morningstar
Gold in the Garden

ChariotVICTOR
◆ P U B L I S H I N G ◆
A DIVISION OF COOK COMMUNICATIONS

Home on Stoney Creek

"Kentucky! Why do we have to move to Kentucky?"

The cry for freedom is spreading throughout the colonies calling many people to war, but not Sarah's family. The cry they hear leads them to a new, untamed wilderness called Kentucky.

Sleeping on pine boughs covered with deerskins, having no one her age to talk to, fighting off pig-eating bears—Kentucky doesn't feel much like freedom to Sarah. She can't understand why God didn't answer her prayers to stay in Virginia, but she vows she'll return some day.

Wanda Luttrell was raised and still lives on the banks of Stoney Creek. Wanda and her husband have shared their home on Stoney Creek with their five children.

Be sure to read all the books in Sarah's Journey:
Home on Stoney Creek
Stranger in Williamsburg
Reunion in Kentucky
Also available as an audio book:
Home on Stoney Creek

ChariotVICTOR
PUBLISHING
A DIVISION OF COOK COMMUNICATIONS

Stranger in Williamsburg

"A spy? Gabrielle Can't be a spy!"

The American Revolution is in full swing, and Sarah Moore is caught right in the middle of it. When she returned to Virginia to live with her aunt's family and learn from their tutor, she certainly had no plans to get involved with a possible spy.

With a war going on, her family back in Kentucky, and people choosing sides all around her, Sarah has begun to wonder if she can trust anyone—even God.

Wanda Luttrell was raised and still lives on the banks of Stoney Creek. Wanda and her husband have shared their home on Stoney Creek with their five children.

Be sure to read all the books in Sarah's Journey:
Home on Stoney Creek
Stranger in Williamsburg
Reunion in Kentucky
Also available as an audio book:
Home on Stoney Creek

ChariotVICTOR
PUBLISHING
A DIVISION OF COOK COMMUNICATIONS

Parents

Are you looking for fun ways to bring the Bible to life for your children?

ChariotVictor Publishing has hundreds of books, toys, games, and videos that help teach your children the Bible and show them how to apply it to their everyday lives.

Look for these educational, inspirational, and fun products at your local Christian bookstore.